伊索 著

吳健平 于國畔 譯

AESOP'S FABLES

伊索寓言

商務印書館

本書譯文由上海譯文出版社有限公司授權使用

責任編輯	陳朝暉
裝幀設計	郭梓琪
排　　版	周　榮
責任校對	趙會明
印　　務	龍寶祺

伊索寓言 *Aesop's Fables*

作　　者	伊　索
譯　　者	吳健平　于國畔
出　　版	商務印書館（香港）有限公司
	香港筲箕灣耀興道 3 號東滙廣場 8 樓
	http://www.commercialpress.com.hk
發　　行	香港聯合書刊物流有限公司
	香港新界荃灣德士古道 220－248 號荃灣工業中心 16 樓
印　　刷	永經堂印刷有限公司
	香港新界荃灣德士古道 188－202 號立泰工業中心第 1 座 3 樓
版　　次	2024 年 7 月第 1 版第 1 次印刷
	© 2024 商務印書館（香港）有限公司
	ISBN 978 962 07 0438 3
	Printed in China

Publisher's Note 出版説明

　　《伊索寓言》作為古希臘文學中的瑰寶，以其獨特的寓意性、啟發性和審美價值，歷久彌新，影響深遠。作品匯集了數百篇短小精悍的故事，通過動物、植物等生動的形象，展現了人性的多樣性和社會的複雜性，以小故事講大道理。

　　本次編選的《伊索寓言》共收錄 185 篇經典寓言故事，涵蓋了動物寓言、人物寓言、神話寓言等多種類型，其中不乏一些耳熟能詳的經典篇目，如《狐狸和葡萄》、《農夫和蛇》、《烏龜和兔子》、《烏鴉和水罐》等，同時也加入了一些相對較為冷門但同樣精彩的篇目，以豐富讀者的閱讀選擇。在每篇寓言故事的末尾，還附有簡潔明瞭的寓意解讀，以幫助讀者更好地理解故事內涵。

　　《伊索寓言》不僅是一部文學作品，更是一部智慧的寶庫。它教會我們如何面對生活中的困難和挑戰，如何理解人性的複雜和多樣，以及如何追求真理和美好。無論是青少年還是成年人，都能從中汲取到寶貴的人生經驗和智慧啟示。

商務印書館 (香港) 有限公司
編輯出版部

Contents　目錄

Aesop's Fables

1

The Eagle and the Fox

An eagle and a fox became great friends and determined to live near one another: they thought that the more they saw of each other the better friends they would be. So the eagle built a nest at the top of a high tree, while the fox settled in a thicket at the foot of it and produced a litter of cubs. One day the fox went out foraging for food, and the eagle, who also wanted food for her young, flew down into the thicket, caught up the fox's cubs, and carried them up into the tree for a meal for herself and her family. When the fox came back, and found out what had happened, she was not so much sorry for the loss of her cubs as furious because she couldn't get at the eagle and pay her out for her treachery. So she sat down not far off and cursed her. But it wasn't long before she had her revenge. Some villagers happened to be sacrificing a goat on a neighbouring altar, and the eagle flew down and carried off a piece of burning flesh to her nest. There was a strong wind blowing, and the nest caught fire, with the result that her fledglings fell half-roasted to the ground. Then the fox ran to the spot and devoured them in full sight of the eagle.

This story shows that if you betray friendship, you may evade the vengeance of those who you wrong if they are weak, but ultimately you cannot escape the vengeance of heaven.

The Eagle,
the Jackdaw and the Shepherd

An eagle, dropping suddenly from a high rock, carried off a lamb. A jackdaw saw this, was smitten by a sense of rivalry and determined to do the same. So, with a great deal of noise, he pounced upon a ram. But his claws merely got caught in the think ringlets of the ram's fleece, and no matter how frantically he flapped his wings, he was unable to get free and take flight. Finally the shepherd bestirred himself, hurried up to the jackdaw and got hold of him. He clipped the end of his wings and, when evening fell, he carried him back for his children. The children wanted to know what sort of bird this was. So the shepherd replied, 'As far as I can see, it's a jackdaw, but it would like us to think it's an eagle!'

Just so, to compete with the powerful is not only not worth the effort and labour lost, but also brings mockery and calamity upon us.

3
The Eagle and the Beetle

An eagle was chasing a hare, which was running for dear life and was at her wits' end to know where to turn for help. Presently she espied a beetle, and begged it to aid her. So when the eagle came up the beetle warned her not to touch the hare, which was under its protection. But the eagle never noticed the beetle because it was so small, seized the hare and ate her up. The beetle never forgot this, and used to keep an eye on the eagle's nest, and whenever the eagle laid an egg it climbed up and rolled it out of the nest and broke it. At last the eagle got so worried over the loss of her eggs that she went up to Zeus, who is the special protector of eagles, and begged him to give her a safe place to nest in: so he let her lay her eggs in his lap. But the beetle noticed this and made a ball of dirt the size of an eagle's egg, and flew up and deposited it in Zeus's lap. When Zeus saw the dirt, he stood up to shake it out of his robe, and, forgetting about the eggs, he shook them out too, and they were broken just as before. Ever since then, they say, eagles never lay their eggs at the season when beetles are about.

Even the weakest may find means to avenge a wrong.

4
The Nightingale and the Hawk

A nightingale, sitting aloft upon an oak and singing according to his wont, was seen by a hawk who, being in need of food, swooped down and seized him. The nightingale, about to lose his life, earnestly begged the hawk to let him go, saying that he was not big enough to satisfy the hunger of a hawk who, if he wanted food, ought to pursue the larger birds. The hawk, interrupting him, said, 'I should indeed have lost my senses if I should let go food ready in my hand, for the sake of pursuing birds which are not yet even within sight.'

Don't let the thought of greater things prevent you from enjoying what you already have.

The Goatherd and the Wild Goats

A goatherd, driving his flock from their pasture at eventide, found some wild goats mingled among them, and shut them up together with his own for the night. The next day it snowed very hard, so that he could not take the herd to their usual feeding places, but was obliged to keep them in the fold. He gave his own goats just sufficient food to keep them alive, but fed the strangers more abundantly in the hope of enticing them to stay with him and of making them his own. When the thaw set in, he led them all out to feed, and the wild goats scampered away as fast as they could to the mountains. The goatherd scolded them for their ingratitude in leaving him, when during the storm he had taken more care of them than of his own herd. One of them, turning about, said to him, 'That is the very reason why we are so cautious; for if you yesterday treated us better than the goats you have had so long, it is plain also that if others came after us, you would in the same manner prefer them to ourselves.'

It is unwise to treat old friends badly for the sake of new ones.

6
The Cat and the Birds

A cat heard that the birds in an aviary were ailing. So he got himself up as a doctor, and, taking with him a set of the instruments proper to his profession, presented himself at the door, and inquired after the health of the birds. 'We shall do very well,' they replied, without letting him in, 'when we've seen the last of you.'

A villain may disguise himself, but he will not deceive the wise.

The Fox and the Goat

A fox one day fell into a deep well and could find no means of escape. A boat, overcome with thirst, came to the same well, and seeing the fox, inquired if the water was good. Concealing his sad plight under a merry guise, the fox indulged in a lavish praise of the water, saying it was excellent beyond measure, and encouraging him to descend. The goat, mindful only of his thirst, thoughtlessly jumped down, but just as he drank, the fox informed him of the difficulty they were both in and suggested a scheme for their common escape. 'If,' said he, 'you will place your forefeet upon the wall and bend your head, I will run up your back and escape, and will help you out afterwards.' The goat readily assented and the fox leaped upon his back. Steadying himself with the goat's horns, he safely reached the mouth of the well and made off as fast as he could. When the goat upbraided him for breaking his promise, he turned around and cried out, 'You foolish old fellow! If you had as many brains in your head as you have hairs in your beard, you would never have gone down before you had inspected the way up, nor have exposed yourself to dangers from which you had no means of escape.'

Look before you leap.

The Fox and the Lion

When a fox who had never yet seen a lion, fell in with him by chance for the first time in the forest, he was so frightened that he nearly died with fear. On meeting him for the second time, he was still much alarmed, but not to the same extent as at first. On seeing him the third time, he so increased in boldness that he went up to him and commenced a familiar conversation with him.

Familiarity breeds contempt.

9
The Fox and the Leopard

The fox and the leopard disputed which was the more beautiful of the two. The leopard exhibited one by one the various spots which decorated his skin. But the fox, interrupting him, said, 'And how much more beautiful than you am I, who am decorated, not in body, but in mind.'

A fine coat is not always an indication of an attractive mind.

The Fishermen and the Stone

Some fishermen were out trawling their nets. Perceiving them to be very heavy, they danced about for joy and supposed that they had taken a large catch. When they had dragged the nets to the shore they found but few fish: the nets were full of sand and stones, and the men were beyond measure cast down so much at the disappointment which had befallen them, but because they had formed such very different expectations. One of their company, an old man, said, 'Let us cease lamenting, my mates, for, as it seems to me, sorrow is always the twin sister of joy; and it was only to be looked for that we, who just now were over-rejoiced, should next have something to make us sad.'

The fable shows that we have to endure reversals of fortune, since we know that life is a matter of luck.

11
The Fox and the Monkey

A fox and a monkey were travelling together on the same road. As they journeyed, they passed through a cemetery full of monuments. 'All these monuments which you see,' said the monkey, 'are erected in honour of my ancestors, who were in their day freedmen and citizens of great renown.' The fox replied, 'You have chosen a most appropriate subject for your falsehoods, as I am sure none of your ancestors will be able to contradict you.'

Boasters brag most when they cannot be detected.

The Fox and the Grapes

A famished fox saw some clusters of ripe black grapes hanging from a trellised vine. She resorted to all her tricks to get at them, but wearied herself in vain, for she could not reach them. At last she turned away, hiding her disappointment and saying, 'The grapes are sour, and not ripe as I thought.'

There are many who pretend to despise and belittle that which is beyond their reach.

13
The Cat and the Cock

A cat caught a cock, and pondered how he might find a reasonable excuse for eating him. He accused him of being a nuisance to men by crowing in the nighttime and not permitting them to sleep. The cock defended himself by saying that he did this for the benefit of men, that they might rise in time for their labours. The cat replied, 'Although you abound in specious apologies, I shall not remain supperless'; and he made a meal of him.

The want of a good excuse never kept a villain from crime.

The Fox Without a Tail

It happened that a fox caught its tail in a trap, and in struggling to release himself lost all of it but the stump. At first he was ashamed to show himself among his fellow foxes. But at last he was determined to put a bolder face upon his misfortune, and summoned all the foxes to a general meeting to consider a proposal which he had to place before them. When they had assembled together, the fox proposed that they should all do away with their tails. He pointed out how inconvenient a tail was when they were pursued by their enemies, the dogs; how much it was in the way when they desired to sit down and hold a friendly conversation with one another. He failed to see any advantage in carrying about such a useless encumbrance. 'That is all very well,' said one of the older foxes; 'but I do not think you would have recommended us to dispense with our chief ornament if you had not happened to lose it yourself.'

Do not listen to the advice of him who seeks to lower you to his own level.

15
The Fox and the Crocodile

The fox and the crocodile were disputing about their pedigrees. The crocodile was proudly enumerating the eminent qualities of his ancestors, and when he said that they had been the highest ranking athletic officials, the fox remarked, 'My dear sir, even if you had not mentioned it, the mere condition of your skin is evidence enough that you have suffered long years of athletic sports out of doors in the sun!'

Boasters often themselves prove that what they are saying is wrong.

The Fishermen and the Tuna Fish

Some fishermen had gone out fishing, and when they had struggled for a long time but had not managed to catch anything, they became very downcast and prepared to turn back. All of a sudden a tuna fish who was being chased by some bigger fish leaped into their boat. The men seized the tuna fish and went home rejoicing.

The story shows that Luck often bestows the things that skill cannot obtain.

17
The Fox and the Woodcutter

A fox, running before the hounds, came across a woodcutter felling an oak and begged him to show him a safe hiding-place. The woodcutter advised him to take shelter in his own hut, so the Fox crept in and hid himself in a corner. The huntsman soon came up with his hounds and inquired of the woodcutter if he had seen the fox. He declared that he had not seen him, and yet pointed, all the time he was speaking, to the hut where the fox lay hidden. The huntsman took no notice of the signs, but believing his word, hastened forward in the chase. As soon as they were well away, the fox departed without taking any notice of the woodcutter: whereon he called to him and reproached him, saying, 'You ungrateful fellow, you owe your life to me, and yet you leave me without a word of thanks.' The fox replied, 'Indeed, I should have thanked you fervently if your deeds had been as good as your words, and if your hands had not been traitors to your speech.'

There is as much malice in a wink as in a word.

The Swollen Fox

A starving fox found in a hollow tree a quantity of bread and meat, which some shepherds had placed there against their return. Delighted with his find he slipped in through the narrow aperture and greedily devoured it all. But when he tried to get out again he found himself so swollen after his big meal that he could not squeeze through the hole, and fell to whining and groaning over his misfortune. Another fox, happening to pass that way, came and asked him what the matter was; and, on learning the state of the case, said, 'Well, my friend, I see nothing for it but for you to stay where you are till you shrink to your former size; you'll get out then easily enough.'

This fable shows that time resolves difficulties.

19
The Halcyon and the Sea

The halcyon is a bird who is fond of deserted places and who always lives on the sea. They say that she makes her nest on the rocky cliffs of the coast in order to protect herself from human hunters. So when a certain halcyon was about to lay her eggs, she went to a promontory and found a rock jutting out towards the sea and decided to make her nest there. But when she went to look for food, it happened that the sea swelled under the blustering wind and reached as high as the halcyon's home and flooded the nest, killing her chicks. When the halcyon returned and saw what had happened, she said, 'What a fool I was to have protected myself against a plot hatched on the land by taking refuge here on the sea, when it is the sea that has utterly betrayed me!'

There are people who do the same thing: while defending themselves against their enemies, they unwittingly fall prey to friends who turn out to be far more dangerous.

The Fisherman Who Beat the Water

A fisherman was fishing in a river. He had stretched his nets across and dammed the current from one bank to the other. Then, having attached a stone to the end of a flaxen rope, he beat the water with it, so that the fish would panic and throw themselves into the mesh of the net as they fled. One of the locals from the vicinity saw him doing this and reproached him for disturbing the river and making them have to drink muddied water. The fisherman replied, 'But if the river is not disturbed, I shall be forced to die of hunger.'

It is like this in a city-state: the demagogues thrive by throwing the state into discord.

21
The Fox and the Mask

A fox, having crept into an actor's house, rummaged through his wardrobe and found, among other things, a large, beautifully fashioned mask of a monster. He held it in his paws and exclaimed, 'Ah! What a head! But it hasn't got a brain!'

This fable refers to men who have magnificent bodies but poor judgment.

22
The Cheat

A poor man, being very ill and getting worse, promised the gods to sacrifice to them one hundred oxen if they saved him from death. The gods, wishing to put him to the test, restored him to health very quickly. Soon he was up and out of bed. But, as he didn't really have any oxen, he modeled one hundred of them out of tallow and burned them on an altar, saying, 'Receive my votive offering, oh gods!' But the gods, wanting to trick him in their turn, sent him a dream saying g that if he would go to the seashore it would result in one thousand Athenian drachmas for him. Unable to contain his joy, he ran to the beach, where he came across some pirates who took him away and sold him into slavery. And they did indeed obtain one thousand Athenian drachmas for him.

This fable is well applied to a liar.

23
The Charcoal-Burner and the Fuller

A charcoal-burner carried on his trade in his own house. One day he met a friend, a fuller, and entreated him to come and live with him, saying that they should be far better neighbours and that their housekeeping expenses would be lessened. The fuller replied, 'The arrangement is impossible as far as I am concerned, for whatever I should whiten, you would immediately blacken again with your charcoal.'

The story shows that opposites are utterly incompatible. Like will draw like.

Athena and the Shipwreck

A rich man of Athens was making a voyage across the sea. In a fierce storm, the winds and waves broke the ship to pieces. All the passengers were thrown into the water and had to swim for their lives. The rich man, however, did not swim. Instead, he called upon Athena, goddess of his city. 'O Athena, I'll give you a thousand gold pieces if you rescue me from the sea.' One of the ship's sailors swam by and shouted at him, 'While you bargain with Athena, you should also try swimming!'

The goddess helps those who help themselves.

25
The Manslayer

A man committed a murder, and was pursued by the relations of the man whom he murdered. On his reaching the river Nile he saw a lion on its bank and being fearfully afraid, climbed up a tree. He found a serpent in the upper branches of the tree, and again being greatly alarmed, he threw himself into the river, where a crocodile caught him and ate him. Thus the earth, the air, and the water alike refused shelter to a murderer.

Evil meets evil end.

The Man Who Promised the Impossible

A poor man was very ill, and not expected to live. As the doctors were about to give up hope for him, he appealed to the gods, promising to offer up to them a hecatomb and to consecrate to them some votive offerings if he recovered. The man's wife who was at his side, asked him, 'And where are you going to get the money to pay for all that?' The man told her, 'Do you think I might get better so that the gods can call me to account?'

This fable shows that men readily make promises which in reality they have no intention of keeping.

27
The Man and the Satyr

A long time ago a man met a Satyr in the forest and succeeded in making friends with him. The two soon became the best of comrades, living together in the man's hut. But one cold winter evening, as they were walking homeward, the Satyr saw the man blow on his fingers. 'Why do you do that?' asked the Satyr. 'To warm my hands,' the man replied. When they reached home the man prepared two bowls of porridge. These he placed steaming hot on the table, and the comrades sat down very cheerfully to enjoy the meal. But much to the Satyr's surprise, the man began to blow into his bowl of porridge. 'Why do you do that?' he asked. 'To cool my porridge,' replied the man. The Satyr sprang hurriedly to his feet and made for the door. 'Goodbye,' he said, 'I've seen enough. A fellow that blows hot and cold in the same breath cannot be friends with me!'

The man who talks for both sides is not to be trusted by either.

28
The Blind Man and the Cub

There was once a blind man who had so fine a sense of touch that, when any animal was put into his hands, he could tell what it was merely by the feel of it. One day the cub of a wolf was put into his hands, and he was asked what it was. He felt it for some time, and then said, 'Indeed, I am not sure whether it is a wolf's cub or a fox's. But this I know—it would never do to trust it in a sheepfold.'

Evil tendencies are early shown.

29
The Astronomer

An astronomer used to go out at night to observe the stars. One evening, as he wandered through the suburbs with his whole attention fixed on the sky, he fell accidentally into a deep well. While he lamented and bewailed his sores and bruises, and cried loudly for help, a neighbour ran to the well, and learning what had happened said, 'Hark ye, old fellow, why, in striving to pry into what is in heaven, do you not manage to see what is on earth?'

Take care of the little things and the big things will take care of themselves.

30
The Farmer and His Sons

A farmer, being at death's door, and desiring to impart to his sons a secret of much moment, called them round him and said, 'My sons, I am shortly about to die; I would have you know, therefore, that in my vineyard there lies a hidden treasure. Dig, and you will find it.' As soon as their father was dead, the sons took spade and fork and turned up the soil of the vineyard over and over again, in their search for the treasure which they supposed to lie buried there. They found none, however. But the vines, after so thorough a digging, produced a crop such as had never before been seen.

Industry is itself a treasure.

The Frogs

Two frogs lived together in a marsh. But one hot summer the marsh dried up, and they left it to look for another place to live in: for frogs like damp places if they can get them. By and by they came to a deep well, and one of them looked down into it, and said to the other, 'This looks a nice cool place. Let us jump in and settle here.' But the other, who had a wiser head on his shoulders, replied, 'Not so fast, my friend. Supposing this well dried up like the marsh, how should we get out again?'

Think twice before you act.

32
The North Wind and the Sun

A dispute arose between the north wind and the sun, each claiming that he was stronger than the other. At last they agreed to try their powers upon a traveller, to see which could soonest strip him of his cloak. The north wind had the first try; and, gathering up all his force for the attack, he came whirling furiously down upon the man, and caught up his cloak as though he would wrest it from him by one single effort. But the harder he blew, the more closely the man wrapped it round himself.

Then came the turn of the sun. At first he beamed gently upon the traveller, who soon unclasped his cloak and walked on with it hanging loosely about his shoulders. Then he shone forth in his full strength, and the man, before he had gone many steps, was glad to throw his cloak right off and complete his journey more lightly clad.

Persuasion is better than force.

33
The Cage-Bird and the Bat

A singing-bird was confined in a cage which hung outside a window, and had a way of singing at night when all other birds were asleep. One night a bat came and clung to the bars of the cage, and asked the bird why she was silent by day and sang only at night. 'I have a very good reason for doing so,' said the bird, 'it was once when I was singing in the daytime that a fowler was attracted by my voice, and set his nets for me and caught me. Since then I have never sung except by night.' But the bat replied, 'It is no use your doing that now when you are a prisoner: if only you had done so before you were caught, you might still have been free.'

Precautions are useless after the event.

The Farmer and His Dogs

There was a farmer who was trapped on his country estate by a winter storm. He didn't have any food, so first he ate his sheep, then his goats. When the storm got worse, he even slaughtered the oxen who pulled his plow. When the dogs saw what was happening, they said to one another, 'Let's get out of here now! Since we can see that the master didn't even spare the oxen who labour on his behalf, how can we expect to be spared?'

The story shows that you should especially avoid someone who does not even spare his own people.

35
The Bundle of Sticks

A certain man had several sons who were always quarrelling with one another, and, try as he might, he could not get them to live together in harmony. So he determined to convince them of their folly by the following means. Bidding them fetch a bundle of sticks, he invited each in turn to break it across his knee. All tried and all failed. And then he undid the bundle, and handed them the sticks one by one, when they had no difficulty at all in breaking them. 'There, my boys,' said he, 'united you will be more than a match for your enemies. But if you quarrel and separate, your weakness will put you at the mercy of those who attack you.'

Union is strength.

The Mistress and Her Servants

A widow, thrifty and industrious, had two servants, whom she kept pretty hard at work. They were not allowed to lie long abed in the mornings, but the old lady had them up and doing as soon as the cock crew. They disliked intensely having to get up at such an hour, especially in winter-time: and they thought that if it were not for the cock waking up their mistress so horribly early, they could sleep longer. So they caught it and wrung its neck. But they weren't prepared for the consequences. For what happened was that their mistress, not hearing the cock crow as usual, waked them up earlier than ever, and set them to work in the middle of the night.

This fable shows that, for many people, it is their own devices that are the cause of their misery.

37
The Sorceress

A sorceress made a profession of supplying charms and spells for the appeasing of the anger of the gods. She was assiduous in her business and thus made a very comfortable living. But, envious of her success, someone accused her of making innovations in religion, and prosecuted her for it in court. Her accusers succeeded and had her condemned to death. As she was led away from the court, someone shouted to her, 'Hey, woman! You made such a profit from diverting the wrath of the gods! Why can't you divert the wrath of the people?'

This fable applies as well to a wandering seeress who promises wonders but shows herself incapable of ordinary things.

The Old Woman and the Doctor

An old woman became almost totally blind from a disease of the eyes, and, after consulting a doctor, made an agreement with him in the presence of witnesses that she should pay him a high fee if he cured her, while if he failed he was to receive nothing. The doctor accordingly prescribed a course of treatment, and every time he paid her a visit he took away with him some article out of the house, until at last, when he visited her for the last time, and the cure was complete, there was nothing left. When the old woman saw that the house was empty she refused to pay him his fee; and, after repeated refusals on her part, he sued her before the magistrates for payment of her debt. On being brought into court she was ready with her defence. 'The claimant,' said she, 'has stated the facts about our agreement correctly. I undertook to pay him a fee if he cured me, and he, on his part, promised to charge nothing if he failed. Now, he says I am cured; but I say that I am blinder than ever, and I can prove what I say. When my eyes were bad I could at any rate see well enough to be aware that my house contained a certain amount of furniture and other things; but now, when according to him I am cured, I am entirely unable to see anything there at all.'

Thus it is that dishonest people, thinking only of their greed, furnish evidence of their own guilt.

39
The Orator Demades

The orator Demades spoke one day to the people of Athens. As no one was taking much notice of what he was saying, someone asked if he could tell one of Aesop's fables. Agreeing to the request he commenced thus, 'The goddess Demeter, the swallow and the eel all took the same route. They arrived at the edge of a river. Then the swallow flew up into the air and the eel dived into the water.' At the point he stopped speaking. 'And Demeter?' someone asked, 'What did she do?' 'She got angry with you,' he replied, 'who are neglecting the affairs of the state to listen to the fables of Aesop.'

Thus men are unreasonable who neglect important things in preference to things which give them pleasure.

The Two Travellers and the Bear

Two men were travelling in company through a forest, when, all at once, a huge bear crashed out of the brush near them. One of the men, thinking of his own safety, climbed a tree. The other, unable to fight the savage beast alone, threw himself on the ground and lay still, as if he were dead. He had heard that a bear will not touch a dead body. It must have been true, for the bear snuffed at the man's head awhile, and then, seeming to be satisfied that he was dead, walked away. The man in the tree climbed down. 'It looked just as if that bear whispered in your ear,' he said. 'What did he tell you?' 'He said,' answered the other, 'that it was not at all wise to keep company with a fellow who would desert his friend in a moment of danger.'

Misfortune tests the sincerity of friendship.

41

The Two Travellers and the Axe

Two men were journeying together. One of them picked up an axe that lay upon the path, and said, 'I have found an axe.' 'Nay, my friend,' replied the other, 'do not say "I," but "We" have found an axe.' They had not gone far before they saw the owner of the axe pursuing them, and he who had picked up the axe said, 'We are undone.' 'Nay,' replied the other, 'keep to your first mode of speech, my friend; what you thought right then, think right now. Say "I," not "We" are undone.'

He who shares the danger ought to share the prize.

42
The Bee-Keeper

A thief found his way into an apiary when the bee-keeper was away, and stole all the honey. When the keeper returned and found the hives empty, he was very much upset and stood staring at them for some time. Before long the bees came back from gathering honey, and, finding their hives overturned and the keeper standing by, they made for him with their stings. At this he fell into a passion and cried, 'You ungrateful scoundrels, you let the thief who stole my honey get off scot-free, and then you go and sting me who have always taken such care of you!'

When you hit back make sure you have got the right man.

43
The Stag at the Pool

A thirsty stag went down to a pool to drink. As he bent over the surface he saw his own reflection in the water, and was struck with admiration for his fine spreading antlers, but at the same time he felt nothing but disgust for the weakness and slenderness of his legs. While he stood there looking at himself, he was seen and attacked by a lion; but in the chase which ensued, he soon drew away from his pursuer, and kept his lead as long as the ground over which he ran was open and free of trees. But coming presently to a wood, he was caught by his antlers in the branches, and fell a victim to the teeth and claws of his enemy. 'Woe is me!' he cried with his last breath, 'I despised my legs, which might have saved my life; but I gloried in my horns, and they have proved my ruin.'

What is worth most is often valued least.

44
The Sea Voyagers

Some people boarded a ship and took to sea. When they were out in the open, a violent storm blew up and the vessel was in danger of sinking. One by one the passengers tore at their clothes, invoking the gods of their countries with tears and moans and promising to make offerings of thanks if they escaped and the boat was saved. But the tempest stopped and calm was restored. So they began to make merry, to dance, to leap about like people do who have escaped from an unforeseen danger. Then the stout-spirited steersman sprang up and said to them, 'My friends, let us rejoice, but let us do so like people who may yet again encounter the storm.'

The fable shows that you shouldn't become too elated with success, and that you should remember the fickleness of chance.

The Fox and the Monkey

At a gathering of all the animals the monkey danced and delighted them so much that they made him their king. The fox, however, was very much disgusted at the promotion of the monkey: so having one day found a trap with a piece of meat in it, he took the monkey there and said to him, 'Here is a dainty morsel I have found, sire; I did not take it myself, because I thought it ought to be reserved for you, our king. Will you be pleased to accept it?' The monkey made at once for the meat and got caught in the trap. Then he bitterly reproached the fox for leading him into danger; but the fox only laughed and said, 'O monkey, you call yourself king of the beasts and haven't more sense than to be taken in like that!'

The true leader proves himself by his qualities.

46
The Two Dung Beetles

There was a bull who was pastured on a little island. Two dung beetles lived there too, feeding on the bull's manure. Winter was approaching, so one of the dung beetles said to the other, 'I want to go to the mainland and I will live there by myself during the winter. If I happen to find a good feeding ground over there, I bring back something for you too.' The beetle then moved to the mainland and found a lot of manure that was all moist and fresh. He settled in and had plenty to eat. When winter was over, he flew back to the little island where he had left the first beetle. When the first beetle saw that the second beetle was coming back looking so plump and fat, he asked him why he had not done what he had promised. The second beetle replied, 'Don't blame me! It's the nature of the place: there is plenty to eat there, but the food cannot be taken away.'

This story fits those people who make displays of friendship at the height of the party, but who are otherwise useless to their friends.

The Goose That Laid the Golden Eggs

There was once a countryman who possessed the most wonderful goose you can imagine, for every day when he visited the nest, the goose had laid a beautiful, glittering, golden egg. The countryman took the eggs to market and soon began to get rich. But it was not long before he grew impatient with the goose because she gave him only a single golden egg a day. He was not getting rich fast enough. Then one day, after he had finished counting his money, the idea came to him that he could get all the golden eggs at once by killing the goose and cutting it open. But when the deed was done, not a single golden egg did he find, and his precious goose was dead.

Much wants more and loses all.

48
The Two Dogs

A man had two dogs: a hound, trained to assist him in his sports, and a housedog, taught to watch the house. When he returned home after a good day's sport, he always gave the housedog a large share of his spoil. The hound, feeling much aggrieved at this, reproached his companion, saying, 'It is very hard to have all this labour, while you, who do not assist in the chase, luxuriate on the fruits of my exertions.' The housedog replied, 'Do not blame me, my friend, but find fault with the master, who has not taught me to labour, but to depend for subsistence on the labour of others.'

The moral of the story is: Children are not to be blamed for the faults of their parents.

The Man and His Wife

A man had a wife who made herself hated by all the members of his household. Wishing to find out if she had the same effect on the persons in her father's house, he made some excuse to send her home on a visit to her father. After a short time she returned, and when he inquired how she had got on and how the servants had treated her, she replied, 'The herdsmen and shepherds cast on me looks of aversion.' He said, 'O wife, if you were disliked by those who go out early in the morning with their flocks and return late in the evening, what must have been felt towards you by those with whom you passed the whole day!'

Straws show how the wind blows.

50
The Vain Jackdaw

Zeus announced that he intended to appoint a king over the birds, and named a day on which they were to appear before his throne, when he would select the most beautiful of them all to be their ruler. Wishing to look their best on the occasion they repaired to the banks of a stream, where they busied themselves in washing and preening their feathers. The jackdaw was there along with the rest, and realised that, with his ugly plumage, he would have no chance of being chosen as he was: so he waited till they were all gone, and then picked up the most gaudy of the feathers they had dropped, and fastened them about his own body, with the result that he looked gayer than any of them. When the appointed day came, the birds assembled before Zeus's throne; and, after passing them in review, he was about to make the jackdaw king, when all the rest set upon the king-elect, stripped him of his borrowed plumes, and exposed him for the jackdaw that he was.

Borrowed feathers do not make fine birds.

51
Zeus and the Fox

Zeus had turned the fox into the likeness of a human being and had seated her on the throne as his queen. But when the fox happened to notice a beetle creeping out from its hole, she leaped up and began chasing this familiar object of prey. The gods laughed at the fox as she ran, while the great father of the gods blushed and renounced his relations with the fox. As he chased her out of the chamber, Zeus said, 'Live the life you deserve, since you clearly are not worthy of my favours!'

No piece of luck can conceal a depraved nature.

The Ant and the Dung Beetle

During the summer, the ant went around the fields collecting grains of wheat and barley so that he could store up some food for the winter. A dung beetle watched the ant and decided that he must be a wretched creature since he worked all the time, never taking a moment's rest, unlike the other animals. The ant didn't pay attention to the dung beetle and simply went about his business. When winter came and the dung was washed away by the rain, the beetle grew hungry. He went to the ant and begged him to share a little bit of his food. The ant replied, 'O beetle, if you had done some work yourself instead of making fun of me while I was working so hard, then you would not need to be asking me for food.'

The fable teaches us that we should not neglect important things that require our attention, and instead we should attend in good time to our future well-being.

53
The Tunny-Fish and the Dolphin

A tunny-fish was chased by a dolphin and splashed through the water at a great rate, but the dolphin gradually gained upon him, and was just about to seize him when the force of his flight carried the tunny on to a sandbank. In the heat of the chase the dolphin followed him, and there they both lay out of the water, gasping for dear life. When the tunny saw that his enemy was doomed like himself, he said, 'I don't mind having to die now: for I see that he who is the cause of my death is about to share the same fate.'

The fable shows that people readily undergo a disaster when they can witness the destruction of those who are to blame.

The Doctor at the Funeral

As a doctor was following the funeral cortege of one of his relatives, he remarked to the mourners in the procession that the man would not have died if he had stopped drinking wine and used an enema. Someone in the crowd then said to the doctor, 'Hey! This is hardly the time to offer such advice, when it can't do him any good. You should have given him the advice when he still could have used it!'

The fable shows that friends should offer their help when there is need of it, and not play the wise man after the fact.

55
The Bird Catcher and the Partridge

A bird catcher had captured a partridge and was ready to strangle her right there on the spot. The partridge wanted to save her life so she pleaded with the bird catcher and said, 'If you release me from this snare, I will lure many partridges here and bring them to you.' The bird catcher was made even angrier by this and he killed the partridge immediately.

This fable shows that someone who lays a trap for others will fall victim to it himself.

The Crab and the Fox

A crab once left the sea-shore and went and settled in a meadow some way inland, which looked very nice and green and seemed likely to be a good place to feed in. But a hungry fox came along and spied the crab and caught him. Just as he was going to be eaten up, the crab said, 'This is just what I deserve; for I had no business to leave my natural home by the sea and settle here as though I belonged to the land.'

Be content with your lot.

57
The Beaver

The beaver is a four-footed animal who lives in pools. A beaver's genitals serve, it is said, to cure certain ailments. So when the beaver is spotted and pursued to be mutilated—since he knows why he is being hunted—he will run for a certain distance, and he will use the speed of his feet to remain intact. But when he sees himself about to be caught, he will bite off his own parts, throw them, and thus save his own life.

Among men also, those are wise who, if attacked for their money, will sacrifice it rather than lose their lives.

The Thieves and the Rooster

Thieves broke into a certain house and didn't find anything inside except a rooster. The thieves grabbed the rooster and made their escape. Later, when they were ready to kill him, the rooster begged the thieves to let him go, claiming that he was useful to people because he woke them to go about their tasks in the dark. The thieves said, 'All the more reason to kill you: when you wake them up, you prevent us from robbing their houses!'

The story shows it is precisely the things that frustrate wicked people which are beneficial to honest folk.

59

The Raven and the Fox

A raven stole a piece of meat and flew up and perched on a branch with it. A fox saw him there and determined to get the meat for himself. So he sat at the base of the tree and said to the raven, 'Of all the birds you are by far the most beautiful. You have such elegant proportions, are so stately and sleek. You were ideally made to be the king of all the birds. And if you only had a voice you would surely be the king.' The raven, wanting to demonstrate to him that there was nothing wrong with his voice, dropped and meat and uttered a great cry. The fox rushed forward, pounced on the meat, and said, 'Oh raven, if only you also had judgment, you would want for nothing to be the king of the birds.'

This fable is a lesson to all fools.

The Jackdaw and the Pigeons

A jackdaw, watching some pigeons in a farmyard, was filled with envy when he saw how well they were fed, and determined to disguise himself as one of them, in order to secure a share of the good things they enjoyed. So he painted himself white from head to foot and joined the flock; and, so long as he was silent, they never suspected that he was not a pigeon like themselves. But one day he was unwise enough to start chattering, when they at once saw through his disguise and pecked him so unmercifully that he was glad to escape and join his own kind again. But the other jackdaws did not recognise him in his white dress, and would not let him feed with them, but drove him away: and so he became a homeless wanderer for his pains.

The story shows that we too must be contented with our lot in life, since being greedy for more is pointless and can even deprive us of the things that are ours.

61

The Hound Who Chased the Lion, and the Fox

A hunting hound, having spotted a lion, set off in pursuit of him. But the lion turned on him and began to roar. Then the dog took fright and turned back. A fox saw this and said to the dog, 'My poor fellow, you chased a lion but you couldn't even endure his roar!'

One could relate this fable with regard to presumptuous people who mix with those more powerful than themselves in order to denigrate them, but then turn and run away when faced by them.

The Dog Who Carried a Meat

A dog was crossing a river holding a piece of meat in his mouth. Catching sight of his reflection in the water, he believed that it was another dog who was holding a bigger piece of meat. So, dropping his own piece, he leaped into the water to take the piece from the other dog. But the result was that he ended up with neither piece—one didn't even exist and the other was swept away by the current.

This fable applies to the covetous.

63

The Sleeping Dog and the Wolf

A dog lay asleep in front of a farm building. A wolf pounced on him and was going to make a meal of him, when the dog begged him not to eat him straight away, 'At the moment,' he said, 'I am thin and lean. But wait a little while; my masters will be celebrating a wedding feast. I will get some good mouthfuls and will fatten up and will be much better meal for you.' The wolf believed him and went on his way. A little while later he came back and found the dog asleep on top of the house. He stopped below and shouted up to him, reminding him of their agreement. The dog said, 'Oh, wolf! If you ever see me asleep in front of the farm again, don't wait for the wedding banquet!'

Once bitten, twice shy.

64
The Hares and the Frogs

Hares, as you know, are very timid. The least shadow, sends them scurrying in fright to a hiding place. Once they decided to die rather than live in such misery. But while they were debating how best to meet death, they thought they heard a noise and in a flash were scampering off to the warren. On the way they passed a pond where a family of frogs was sitting among the reeds on the bank. In an instant the startled frogs were seeking safety in the mud. 'Look,' cried a hare, 'things are not so bad after all, for here are creatures who are even afraid of us!'

However unfortunate we may think we are there is always someone worse off than ourselves.

65

The Lion and the Farmer

A lion fell deeply in love with the daughter of a cottager and wanted to marry her; but her father was unwilling to give her to so fearsome a husband, and yet didn't want to offend the lion; so he hit upon the following expedient. He went to the lion and said, 'I think you will make a very good husband for my daughter, but I cannot consent to your union unless you let me draw your teeth and pare your nails, for my daughter is terribly afraid of them.' The lion was so much in love that he readily agreed that this should be done. When once, however, he was thus disarmed, the cottager was afraid of him no longer, but drove him away with his club.

If you follow your enemies' advice, you will run into danger.

The Old Lion

A lion, enfeebled by age and no longer able to procure food for himself by force, determined to do so by cunning. Betaking himself to a cave, he lay down inside and feigned to be sick. And whenever any of the other animals entered to inquire after his health, he sprang upon them and devoured them. Many lost their lives in this way, till one day a fox called at the cave, and, having a suspicion of the truth, addressed the lion from outside instead of going in, and asked him how he did. He replied that he was in a very bad way. 'But,' said he, 'why do you stand outside? Pray come in.' 'I should have done so,' answered the fox, 'if I hadn't noticed that all the footprints point towards the cave and none the other way.'

Wise men note the indications of dangers and thus avoid them.

67
The Lion and the Bull

A lion saw a fine fat bull pasturing among a herd of cattle and cast about for some means of getting him into his clutches; so he sent him word that he was sacrificing a sheep, and asked if he would do him the honour of dining with him. The bull accepted the invitation, but, on arriving at the lion's den, he saw a great array of saucepans and spits, but no sign of a sheep; so he turned on his heel and walked quietly away. The lion called after him in an injured tone to ask the reason, and the bull turned round and said, 'I have reason enough. When I saw all your preparations it struck me at once that the victim was to be a bull and not a sheep.'

The net is spread in vain in sight of the bird.

The Lion and the Dolphin

A lion was roaming along the seashore when he saw a dolphin raise its head up out of the waves. The lion proposed an alliance of friendship between them. 'You and I are not suited to be friends and allies,' he said, 'for I'm the king of all the beasts on the land and you are the ruler of all the creatures of the sea.' The dolphin willingly agreed. Then, the lion, who had or a long time been at war with a wild bull, called out for the dolphin to come and help him. The dolphin tried to leave the water but failed to do so. The lion accused him of betraying him. But the dolphin replied, 'Don't blame me. Blame Mother Nature. For although she has made me aquatic, she has not allowed me to walk on the land.'

This shows that we too, when we contract alliances, ought to do so with people who can really come to our aid in times of danger.

69
The Lion and the Bear

A lion and a bear, having found the carcass of a faun, were battling over who should have it. They mauled each other so badly that they lost consciousness and lay half-dead. A fox, who happened to pass by and saw them lying there, unable to move,with the faun between them, ran into their midst, grabbed the carcass and escaped with it. The lion and the bear, unable to get up because of the bad state they were in, murmured to each other, 'What fools we are! We've gone to all this trouble just for a fox!'

This fable shows that people have good reason to be annoyed when they see the results of their hard work carried off by chance.

The Lion and the Hare

A lion, having come across a sleeping hare, was about to eat it. But, just at that moment, he caught sight of a deer. So he left the hare and gave chase to the deer. The hare, awoken by the nose, took flight.The lion, having followed the deer for some distance without being able to catch up, went back to the hare. But he found that it had gone. 'It severs me right,' he said. 'I forfeited the meal I had right at hand for the hope of a better catch.'

Thus, at times men, instead of being content with moderate profits, pursue fantastic prospects and, in so doing, foolishly let go of what they have in their hands.

71
The Lion, the Ass and the Fox

The lion, the ass and the fox, having made an agreement together, went off hunting for game. When they had taken plenty of game, the lion asked the ass to divide the spoils between them. The ass divided the food into three equal parts and invited the lion to choose his portion. The lion became enraged, pounced on the ass and devoured him. Then the lion asked the fox to divide the spoils. The fox took all that they had accumulated and gathered it into one large heap, retaining only the tiniest possible morsel for himself. He then invited the lion to choose. The lion then said, 'Well, my good fellow, who taught you to divide so well? You are excellent at it.' The fox replied, 'I learned this technique from the ass's misfortune.'

Learn from the misfortunes of others.

The Lion and the Mouse

Once, a lion was asleep and a mouse ran all along his body. The lion woke up with a start, seized the mouse and was about to eat him, when the mouse begged him to spare his life, promising that he would repay the favour. The lion was so amused at this that he let the little fellow go. Not very long afterwards, the mouse was able to return the favour. For, as a matter of fact, some hunters caught the lion and tied him to a tree with a rope. The mouse heard him groaning, ran up and gnawed through the rope until the lion was free. 'You see?' squeaked the mouse, 'Not long ago you mocked me when I said I would return your favour. But now you can see that even mice are grateful!'

This fable shows how, through the changes of fortune, the strong can come to depend on the weak.

73
The Wolves and the Sheep

Some wolves were trying to surprise a flock of sheep. Unable to be masters of the situation because of the dogs which were guarding them, they resolved to use a ruse to reach their desired end: they sent some delegates to ask the sheep to give up their dogs. It was the dogs, they said, who created the bad blood between them. One only had to surrender the dogs and peace would reign between them. The sheep, not foreseeing what would happen, gave up the dogs. And the wolves, being in control of the situation, easily slaughtered the sheep who were no longer guarded.

This is the case with states: those who easily surrender up their orators cannot doubt that they will very soon be subjugated by their enemies.

The Wolf and the Lamb

A wolf saw a lamb drinking at stream and wanted to devise a suitable pretext for devouring it. So, although he was himself upstream, he accused the lamb of muddying the water and preventing him from drinking. The lamb replied that he only drank with the tip of his tongue and that, besides, being downstream he couldn't muddy the water upstream. The wolf's stratagem having collapsed, he replied, 'But last year you insulted my father.' 'I wasn't even born then,' replied the lamb. So the wolf resumed, 'Whatever you say to justify yourself, I will eat you all the same.'

This fable shows that when some people decided upon doing harm, the fairest defense has no effect whatever.

75
The Wolf and the Crane

A wolf had been feasting too greedily, and a bone had stuck crosswise in his throat. He could get it neither up nor down, and of course he could not eat a thing. Naturally that was an awful state of affairs for a greedy wolf. So away he hurried to the crane. He was sure that she, with her long neck and bill, would easily be able to reach the bone and pull it out. 'I will reward you very handsomely,' said the wolf, 'if you pull that bone out for me.' The crane, as you can imagine, was very uneasy about putting her head in a wolf's throat. But she was grasping in nature, so she did what the wolf asked her to do. When the wolf felt that the bone was gone, he started to walk away. 'But what about my reward!' called the crane anxiously. 'What!' snarled the wolf, whirling around. 'Haven't you got it? Isn't it enough that I let you take your head out of my mouth without snapping it off?'

Expect no reward for serving the wicked.

76
The Wolf and the Goat

A wolf spied a goat grazing above a cave on a sheer cliffface. Unable to reach her, he urged her to come down. For she could, he said, inadvertently fall. Furthermore, the meadow down below, where he was standing, was much better for pasture, for the grass there was lush. But the goat replied, 'It's not for my benefit that you summon me to that pasture; it is because it is you who have nothing to eat.'

Thus, when cunning scoundrels exert their wickedness among people whom they know, they gain nothing by their machinations.

The Fortune-Teller

A fortune-teller, sitting in the marketplace, was telling the fortunes of the passers-by when a person ran up in great haste, and announced to him that the doors of his house had been broken open and that all his goods were being stolen. He sighed heavily and hastened away as fast as he could run. A bystander saw him running and said, 'Oh! You fellow there! How come you to be so good at telling the fortunes of others, and know so little of your own?'

There needs no more than Impudence and Ignorance, on the one side, and a superstitious Credulity on the other, to the setting up of a Fortune-Teller.

78
The Child and the Raven

A woman consulted the diviners about her infant son. They predicted that he would be killed by a raven. Terror-stricken by this prediction, she had a huge chest constructed and shut the boy up inside it to prevent him from being killed by a raven. And every day, at a given time, she opened it and gave the child as much food as he needed. Then, one day when she had opened the chest and was putting back the lid, the child foolishly stuck his head out. So it happened that the handle on the chest fell down on to the top of his head and killed him.

One cannot escape their fate.

The Mice and the Weasels

The mice and the weasels were at war. Now the mice, always seeing themselves beaten, convened a committee, because they imagined that it must be the lack of a leader which caused their setbacks. They elected some generals by raising their hands. Now, the new generals wanted to be distinguished from the ordinary soldiers, so they fashioned some horns and fastened them to their heads. The battle got under way and it happened that the army of the mice was defeated by the weasels. The soldiers fled towards their holes, into which they escaped easily. But the generals, not being able to enter because of their horns getting stuck, were caught and devoured.

Thus, vainglory is often a cause of misfortune.

80
The Castaway and the Sea

A castaway, flung on to the shore, slept from exhaustion. But it wasn't long before he woke and, seeing the sea, reproached her for seducing men with her tranquil air. For then, when she had them in her watery grip, she became wild and caused them to perish. The sea, having taken the form of a woman, said to him, 'But, my friend, it's not up to me. You should instead reproach the winds. For I am naturally as you see me now. It's the winds who, falling on me without a moment's warning, swell me and make me wild.'

Similarly, we ought not to be blamed for being the originators of an injustice when it has been carried out on the order of others, but rather blame should fall on those who have authority over us.

The Bat, the Bramble and the Seagull

The bat, the bramble and the seagull met up with the intention of doing a bit of trading together. The bat went out and borrowed some money to fund the enterprise, the bramble contributed a lot of clothes to be sold and the sesgull brought a large supply of copper to sell. Then they set sail to go trading, but a violent storm arose which capsised their ship and all cargo was lost. They were able to save nothing but themselves from the shipwreck. Ever since that time, the seagull has searched the seashore to see if any of his copper might be washed up somewhere; the bat, fearing his creditors, dare not go out by day and only feeds at night; and the bramble clutches the clothes of all those who pass by, hoping to recognise a familiar piece of material.

This fable shows that we always return to those things in which we have a stake.

82
The Bat and the Weasels

A bat fell to the ground and was caught by a weasel. Realising that she was on the point of being killed, she begged for her life. The weasel said to her that she couldn't let her go, for weasels were supposed to be natural enemies to all birds. The bat replied that she herself was not a bird, but a mouse. She managed to extricate herself from her danger by this means. Eventually, falling a second time, the bat was caught by another weasel. Again she pleaded to the weasel not to eat her. The second weasel declared that she absolutely detested all mice. But the bat positively affirmed that she was not a mouse but a bat. And so she was released again. And that was how she saved herself from death twice by a mere change of name.

Set your sails with the wind. It is not always necessary to confine ourselves to the same tactics. But, on the contrary, if we are adaptable to circumstances we can better escape from danger.

83

The Woodcutter and the Hermes

A woodcutter who was chopping wood on the banks of a river had lost his axe. Not knowing what to do, he sat himself down on the bank and wept. The god Hermes, learning the cause of his distress, took pity on him. Hermes plunged into the river, brought out a golden axe and asked the woodcutter if this were the one which he had lost. The man said, no, that wasn't the one. So Hermes dived back in again and this time he produced a silver axe. But the woodcutter said, no, that wasn't his axe either. Hermes plunged in a third time and brought him his own axe. The man said, yes, indeed, this was the very axe which he had lost. Then Hermes, charmed by his honesty, gave him all three. Returning to his friends, the woodcutter told them about his adventure. One of them took it into his head to get himself some axes as well. So he set off for the riverbank, threw his axe into the current deliberately and then sat down in tears. Then Hermes appeared to him also and, learning the cause of his tears, he dived in and brought him to a golden axe, asking if it were the one which he had lost. The man, all joyful, cried out, 'Yes! It is indeed the one!' But the god, horrified at such effrontery, not only withheld the golden axe but didn't return the man's own.

This fable shows that the gods favour honest people but are hostile to the dishonest.

The Farmer and the Snake

One winter a farmer found a snake stiff and frozen with cold. He had compassion on it, and taking it up, placed it in his bosom. The snake was quickly revived by the warmth, and resuming its natural instincts, bit its benefactor, inflicting on him a mortal wound. 'Oh,' cried the farmer with his last breath, 'I am rightly served for pitying a scoundrel.'

Do not take pity on a scoundrel. The greatest kindness will not bind the ungrateful.

85
The Travellers

Two travellers, journeying along the seashore, climbed to the summit of a tall cliff, and looking over the sea, saw in the distance what they thought was a large ship. They waited in the hope of seeing it enter the harbour, but as the object on which they looked was driven nearer to shore by the wind, they found that it could at the most be a small boat, and not a ship. When however it reached the beach, they discovered that it was only a large faggot of sticks, and one of them said to his companion, 'We have waited for no purpose, for after all there is nothing to see but a load of wood.'

Our mere anticipations of life outrun its realities. Do not let your hopes carry you away from reality.

The Ass Carrying a Load of Salt

An ass with a load of salt was crossing a stream. He slipped and fell into the water. Then the salt dissolved, and when he got up his load was lighter than before, so he was delighted. Another time, when he arrived at the bank of a stream with a load of sponges, he thought that if he fell into the water again when he got up the load would be lighter. So he slipped on purpose. But, of course, the sponges swelled up with the water and the ass was unable to get up again, so he drowned and perished.

The same measures will not suit all circumstances. It is sometimes that people don't suspect that it is their own tricks which land them in disaster.

87

The Ass Carrying a Statue of God

An ass, who was carrying a statue of god on its back, was being
led into the town by a man. As the passers-by prostrated
themselves in front of the statue, the ass imagined that it was he
to whom they were making obeisance and, in his pride, he started
to bray and refused to go any further. The ass-driver, guessing his
thoughts, beat him with his club and said, 'Poor, brainless wretch!
That really would be the limit, to see an ass adored by men.'

*This fable shows that people who take an empty pride in the advantages
of others become a laughing stock to those who know them.*

The Ass and the Cicadas

Hearing some cicadas sing, an ass was charmed by their harmony and envied them their talent. 'What do you eat,' he asked them, 'that gives you such a beautiful song?' 'The dew,' they replied. From then on, the ass waited for the dew and eventually starved to death.

So, when we long for things which are not in our nature, not only will we never be satisfied but we will bring upon ourselves even more misfortune.

89

The Ass and the Wolf

An ass grazing in a small meadow saw a wolf creep up on him, so he pretended to be lame. The wolf, coming nearer, asked why he was limping. The ass replied that he had been jumping over a fence and had landed on a thorn. He advised the wolf to pull it out before eating him to avoid piercing his mouth. The wolf let himself be persuaded. While he was lifting up the ass's foot and concentrating on the hoof, the ass, with a sharp kick in the jaw, knocked his teeth out. As soon as he could speak the wolf growled to himself, 'It serves me right: my father taught me to kill, and I ought to have stuck to that trade instead of attempting to cure.'

Stick to your trade. People who undertake things which are outside their abilities naturally bring themselves to disgrace.

The Ass, the Fox and the Lion

An ass and a fox went into partnership and sallied out to forage for food together. They hadn't gone far before they saw a lion coming their way, at which they were both dreadfully frightened. But the fox thought he saw a way of saving his own skin, and went boldly up to the lion and whispered in his ear, 'I'll manage that you shall get hold of the ass without the trouble of stalking him, if you'll promise to let me go free.' The lion agreed to this, and the fox then rejoined his companion and contrived before long to lead him by a hidden pit, which some hunter had dug as a trap for wild animals, and into which he fell. When the lion saw that the ass was safely caught and couldn't get away, it was to the fox that he first turned his attention, and he soon finished him off, and then at his leisure proceeded to feast upon the ass.

Betray a friend, and you'll often find you have ruined yourself.

91
The Bird Catcher and the Stork

A bird catcher, having laid some nets for cranes, watched his bait from a distance. Then a stork landed in the midst of the cranes and the bird catcher ran back and caught her as well. She begged him to release her, saying that, far from harming men, she was very useful, for she ate snakes and other reptiles. The bird catcher replied, 'If you really are harmless, then you deserve punishment anyway, for landing among the wicked.'

We, too, ought to flee from the company of wicked people so that no one takes us for the accomplice of their wrongdoings.

The Camel

When they first set eyes on a camel, men were afraid. Awed by its huge size, they ran away. But when, in time, they realised its gentleness, they plucked up enough courage to approach it. Then gradually realising that it had no temper, they went up to it and grew to hold it in such contempt that they put a bridle on it and gave it to the children to lead.

This fable shows that habit can overcome the fear which awesome things inspire.

93
The Child Thief and His Mother

A child stole the writing-tablet of his fellow pupil at school and brought it home to his mother. Instead of chastising him, she praised him. And another time he stole a cloak and gave it to her and she praised him even more. Later, coming of age and becoming a young man, he brought her ever more important stolen goods. But, one day, he was caught in the act. His hands were tied behind his back and he was led off to the executioner. His mother went with him and beat her chest. He declared that he would like to whisper something in her ear. As soon as she bent to listen, he grabbed her ear lobe and severed it with one bite of his teeth. She reproached him for his impiety: not content with the crimes he had already committed, he went on to mutilate his mother! He replied, 'If from the time I brought you the first writing-tablet that I stole, you had thrashed me, I would not have come to this pass where I am now: I would not be being led to my death.'

This fable shows that those who are not reprimanded from the outset grow up and get worse.

94

The Monkey and the Fishermen

A monkey perching in a lofty tree saw some fishermen casting their drag-net into a river and watched what they did. Later, leaving their net, they withdrew a short distance to have their lunch. Then the monkey, climbing down from the tree, tried to do what they did, for this animal, it is said, has a natural aptitude for mimicry. But, as soon as he touched the net, he got caught up in it and was in danger of drowning. He then said, 'I only got what I deserve; why have I taken up fishing without having learned how to first?'

This fable shows that by meddling in affairs which one doesn't understand, not only does one gain nothing, but one also does oneself harm.

The Shepherd and the Sheep

A shepherd driving his sheep to a wood, saw an oak of unusual size full of acorns, and spreading his cloak under the branches, he climbed up into the tree and shook them down. The sheep eating the acorns inadvertently frayed and tore the cloak. When the shepherd came down and saw what was done, he said, 'O you most ungrateful creatures! You provide wool to make garments for all other men, but you destroy the clothes of him who feeds you.'

The fable shows that people frequently do favours for someone who has nothing to do with them, while treating their own family members unkindly.

96
The Joking Shepherd

A shepherd who led his flock rather far from the village frequently indulged in the following practical joke. He called to the people of the village to help him, crying that wolves were attacking his sheep. Two or three times. The villagers were alarmed and rushed forth, then returned home having been fooled. But, in the end, it happened that some wolves really did appear. While they ravaged the flock, the shepherd called out for help to the villagers. But they, imagining that he was hoaxing them as usual, didn't bother with him. So it was that he lost his sheep.

This fable shows that liars gain only one thing, which is not to be believed even when they tell the truth.

The Mole

A mole, a creature blind from birth, once said to his mother, 'I am sure that I can see, mother!' In the desire to prove to him his mistake, his mother placed before him a few grains of frankincense, and asked, 'What is it?' The young mole said, 'It is a pebble.' His mother exclaimed, 'My son, I am afraid that you are not only blind, but that you have lost your sense of smell.'

Boast of one thing and you will be found lacking in that and a few other things as well.

98
The Wasp and the Snake

A wasp seated himself upon the head of a snake and, striking him unceasingly with his stings, wounded him to death. The snake, being in great torment and not knowing how to rid himself of his enemy, saw a wagon heavily laden with wood, and went and purposely placed his head under the wheels, saying, 'At least my enemy and I shall perish together.'

This is a fable for people who share their troubles with their enemies.

The Monkey's Children

The monkeys, it is said, give birth to two children at once. Of these two children the mother cherishes and feeds one with tender care, whereas she despises and neglects the other one. So it happens that, by divine fate, the little one that the mother takes care of with love and clasps in her arms is suffocated to death by her, and the one she neglects reaches a perfect maturity.

This fable shows that chance is more powerful than forethought.

100
The Peacock and the Jackdaw

The birds were consulting together on the choice of a king. The peacock demanded to be named king by virtue of his beauty. And the birds were about to vote for him when the jackdaw called out, 'But if you reign, what help can we expect from you when the eagles comes hunting for us?'

This fable shows that you should not reprimand those who, foreseeing future dangers, take precautions in advance.

The Camel, the Elephant and the Monkey

The dumb beasts wanted to elect a king from amongst their ranks. The camel and the elephant were the two leading candidates because of their size and their strength. The monkey, however, argued that they were both unqualified. 'The camel cannot rule us because she doesn't have the guts to fight against those who step out of line,' said the monkey, 'and there is also a potential danger if the elephant is king: how will he defend us from the little pigs?'

The fable shows that great achievements are often blocked by some small thing which prevents their realisation.

102
The Wild Boar and the Fox

The wild boar was standing beside a tree, sharpening his tusks. The fox asked him why he was sharpening his tusks now, when there was no immediate need for him to do so. The wild boar replied, 'I have my reasons! This way, when danger threatens, I won't have to take time to whet my tusks but will instead have them ready for use.'

Preparedness for war is the best guarantee of peace.

The Miser

A miser sold all that he had and bought a lump of gold, which he buried in a hole in the ground by the side of an old wall and went to look at daily. One of his workmen observed his frequent visits to the spot and decided to watch his movements. He soon discovered the secret of the hidden treasure, and digging down, came to the lump of gold, and stole it. The miser, on his next visit, found the hole empty and began to tear his hair and to make loud lamentations. A neighbour, seeing him overcome with grief and learning the cause, said, 'Don't take it so much to heart, my friend; put a stone into the hole, and take a look at it every day: you won't be any worse off than before, for even when you had your gold it was of no earthly use to you.'

A possession is worth no more than the use we make of it.

104
The Hare and the Tortoise

The hare laughed at the tortoise's feet but the tortoise declared, 'I will beat you in a race!' The hare replied, 'Those are just words. Race with me, and you'll see! Who will mark out the track and serve as our umpire?' 'The fox,' replied the tortoise, 'since she is honest and highly intelligent.' When the time for the race had been decided upon, the tortoise did not delay, but immediately took off down the race course. The hare, however, lay down to take a nap, confident in the speed of his feet. Then, when the hare eventually made his way to the finish line, he found that the tortoise had already won.

The story shows that many people have good natural abilities which are ruined by idleness; on the other hand, sobriety, zeal and perseverance can prevail over indolence.

The Swallow and the Serpent

A swallow who had nested inside a court of justice had flown off for a while. A serpent crept up and gobbled up her little ones. Finding the nest empty upon her return, she wailed, beside herself with grief. To console her another swallow told her that she wasn't the only one to have had the misfortune to lose her babies. 'Ah!' she replied, 'I am less distressed to have lost my young than that I should be a victim of a crime in a place where victims of violence should find help.'

This fable shows that ill luck or calamity is often more difficult to bear when it comes from those from whom one least expects it.

106
The Geese and the Cranes

Some wild geese and cranes were foraging for food in the same wet grassland when hunters suddenly appeared. The cranes flew off lightly but the geese, hindered by the heaviness of their bodies, were caught.

It is also like this with people: when a city is taken in war, the poor people easily save themselves by migrating from one land to another, thus preserving their liberty. But the rich are held back by the weight of their wealth and often become enslaved.

The Swallow and the Crow

The swallow and the crow had a contention about their plumage. The crow put an end to the dispute by saying, 'Your feathers are all very well in the spring, but mine protect me against the winter.'

Fair weather friends are not worth much.

108
The Tortoise and the Eagle

A tortoise begged an eagle to teach him to fly. The eagle pointed out that he was not made to fly—far from it! But the tortoise only pleaded with him even more. So the eagle took him in his talons, flew up into the air and then let him go. The tortoise fell on to the rocks and was smashed to pieces.

This fable shows that often, in wanting to compete with others in spite of wiser council, we can do ourselves harm.

109
The Foxes at the River

There were once some foxes who had gathered together on the banks of the River Meander looking for a drink of water. They encouraged one another to approach the river, but no one dared to get too close because of the rushing current. Then one of the foxes came forward in order to embarrass her fellow foxes. Laughing at their cowardice and convinced that she was braver than the rest, she boldly leaped into the water. As the current carried her out into the middle of the river her companions stood on the riverbank and shouted at her, 'Don't leave us! Come back and show us how to get down to the water so that we can also take a drink.' The fox replied as she was being swept downstream, 'I've got a message to take to Miletus, and I need to carry it there. When I come back I will show you!'

This is a story for people who get themselves into trouble because of their boasting.

110
The Swan

The swan is said to sing but once in its life—when it knows that it is about to die. A certain man chanced upon a swan that was for sale and bought it, since he had heard that swans sing very beautifully. At the man's next dinner party, he came and got the swan, expecting that the bird would serenade his guests at dinner. The swan, however, was completely silent. Later on, when the swan realised that it was about to die, it began to sing its funeral dirge. When its owner heard it, he said, 'Well, if you are going to sing this song only at the moment of your death, then I was a fool for having commanded you to do it. I should have ordered you to be butchered instead!'

Some people are the same way: they will agree to do things under compulsion that they are not willing to do as a favour.

The Wolf and the Shepherd

A wolf followed a flock of sheep without doing them any harm. At first the shepherd was fearful of it as an enemy and watched it nervously. But, as the wolf kept on following without making any attempt to harm them, he began to look upon it as more of a guardian than an enemy to be wary of. As he needed to go into town one day, he left the sheep with the wolf in attendance. The wolf, seeing his opportunity, hurled himself at the sheep and tore most of them to pieces. When the shepherd returned and saw the lost sheep he cried out, 'It serves me right. How could I have entrusted my sheep to a wolf?'

It is the same with men: when you entrust valuables to greedy people it is natural that you will lose things.

112
The Ant and the Pigeon

An ant was thirsty and went down to a spring expecting to take a drink of water, but instead he found himself in danger of drowning. A pigeon snapped off a leaf from a nearby tree and threw it to the ant so that he could save himself by climbing up onto the leaf. Meanwhile, a bird catcher showed up and prepared his limed reeds, intending to capture the pigeon. The ant then bit the bird catcher on the foot which caused the bird catcher to shake his limed reeds, warning the pigeon who flew off to safety.

A kindness is never wasted.

The Travellers and the Raven

Some people, travelling on business, came across a one-eyed raven. They turned to look at it and one of them advised that they retrace their steps, it being a bad omen in his opinion. But another of the men spoke up, 'How can this bird predict the future for us when he couldn't predict his own and avoid the loss of his eye?'

Likewise, people who are blinded by their own interests are poorly qualified to give counsel to their neighbours.

114

The Ass Bought in the Market

A man who intended to buy an ass took it on trial and led it to the manger to mix with his others. But the ass, turning its back on the others, went and stood beside the laziest and fattest of the lot. As it stood there and did nothing, the man put a halter on it and led it back to its owner. The owner asked the man if he had given it a fair trial, and he replied, 'I don't need any further trial. I am certain of what he's like because of the companion he chose from among the lot.'

A man is known by the company he keeps.

The Decoys and the Doves

A bird catcher laid out his net, tying some tame doves to the net as decoys. He then stood off at a distance, waiting to see what would happen. Some wild doves flew up to the tame doves and became entangled in the knots of the net. When the bird catcher ran up and began to grab them, the wild doves got angry at the tame doves, since the tame doves had not warned them about the trap even though they were all members of the same species. The tame doves replied, 'Nevertheless, it is better for us to protect the interests of our masters than to please our relations.'

The same is true about household servants: they should not be blamed when their devotion to the master of the house causes them to set aside any loyalty to their kinfolk.

116
The Oath's Punishment

A certain man took a deposit from a friend but intended to keep it for himself. When the depositor then summoned him to swear an oath regarding the deposit, he realised the danger he was in and prepared to leave the city and go to his farm. When he reached the city gates, he saw a lame man who was also on his way out of town. He asked the man who he was and where he was going. The man said that he was the god named Oath and that he was on his way to track down wicked people. The man then asked Oath how often he revisited each city. Oath replied, 'I come back after forty years, or sometimes thirty.' Accordingly, on the very next day the man did not hesitate to swear an oath that he had never received the deposit. But then the man ran into Oath, who dragged him off to the edge of a cliff. The man asked Oath how he could have said that he wasn't coming back for another thirty years when in fact he didn't even grant him a single day's reprieve. Oath explained, 'You also need to know that if somebody intends to provoke me, I am accustomed to come back again the very same day.'

The fable shows that there is no fixed day on which wicked people are punished by the god.

Prometheus and the Making of Man

Following Zeus's orders, Prometheus fashioned humans and animals. When Zeus saw that the animals far outnumbered the humans, he ordered Prometheus to reduce the number of the animals by turning them into people. Prometheus did as he was told, and as a result those people who were originally animals have a human body but the soul of an animal.

This fable is suitable for a man who is rough and brutal.

118
The Cicada and the Fox

A cicada was singing on top of a tall tree. The fox wanted to eat the cicada, so she came up with a trick. She stood in front of the tree and marvelled at the cicada's beautiful song. The fox then asked the cicada to come down and show himself, since the fox wanted to see how such a tiny creature could be endowed with such a sonorous voice. But the cicada saw through the fox's trick. He tore a leaf from the tree and let it fall to the ground. Thinking it was the cicada, the fox pounced and the cicada then said, 'Hey, you must be crazy to think I would come down from here! I've been on my guard against foxes ever since I saw the wings of a cicada in the spoor of a fox.'

The fable shows that a discerning person is made wise by the misfortunes of his neighbours.

The Parrot and the Weasel

A man who had bought a parrot let it fly freely in his house. The parrot, who was tame, jumped up and perched in the hearth and from there began to cackle in a pleasant way. A weasel, seeing him there, asked him who he was and from whence he came. He replied, 'The Master went out to buy me.' The weasel replied, 'And you dare, most shameless creature—newcomer!— to make such sounds, whereas I, who was born in this house, am forbidden by the Master to cry out, and if sometimes I do, he beats me and throws me out of the door!' The parrot replied, 'Oh, go for a long walk! There is no comparison to be made between us. My voice doesn't irritate the master as yours does.'

This fable concerns all malevolent critics who are always ready to throw the blame on to others.

120
The Lioness and the Vixen

A lioness and a vixen were talking together about their young, as mothers will, and saying how healthy and well-grown they were, and what beautiful coats they had, and how they were the image of their parents. 'My litter of cubs is a joy to see,' said the fox; and then she added, rather maliciously, 'But I notice you never have more than one.' 'No,' said the lioness grimly, 'but that one's a lion.'

It is quality, not quantity that counts.

The Lamb Chased by a Wolf

A wolf was chasing a lamb, which took refuge in a temple. The wolf urged it to come out of the precincts, and said, 'If you don't, the priest is sure to catch you and offer you up in sacrifice on the altar.' But the lamb replied, 'Ah well! I would prefer to be a victim of god than to die by your hand.'

This fable shows that if one is being driven towards death, it is better to die with honour.

122
The Donkey and the Mule

A donkey and a mule were walking along together. When the donkey saw that they were carrying equal loads, he got angry and complained that the mule was awarded a double portion of food even though she carried a load that was no bigger than his own. After they had journeyed a little further down the road, the driver saw that the donkey could not hold up under the weight, so he took part of the donkey's load and placed it on the mule. Later, when the driver saw that the donkey had grown even more tired, he again transferred some of the donkey's load to the mule, and so on. Finally the driver took the entire load and shifted it from the donkey to the mule. At that point the mule glanced over at the donkey and said, 'What do you say now: don't I deserve a double portion of food?'

It is the same when we pass judgment on one another's situations: instead of looking at how things start, we should look instead at how they turn out in the end.

The Two Carrying-Pouches

Once upon a time, when Prometheus created men, he hung from them two carrying-pouches. One of these contained the deficiencies of other people and was hung in front. The other contained our own faults, which he suspended behind us. The result of this was that men could see directly down into the pouch containing other people's failings, but were unable to see their own.

One can apply this fable to the muddle-headed person who, blind to his own faults, meddles with those of others which do not concern him at all.

124
The Earthworm and the Snake

An earthworm saw a snake stretched out and envied his length. The earthworm wanted to be as long as that snake, so he lay down beside the snake and tried to extend himself. The worm stretched and stretched until he accidentally split into pieces.

This is what happens to someone who competes with his superiors: he destroys himself before he can equal them.

The Wild Boar,
the Horse and the Huntsman

The wild boar and the horse shared the same pasture. Because the wild boar continually ruined the grass and muddied the water, the horse, wanting to have his revenge, turned to a hunter for help. But the latter announce that he couldn't lend him a hand unless he would agree to wear a bridle and to carry him on his back. The horse yielded to all his demands. Then the huntsman mounted on to his back, took and overcame the board and, leading the horse home, he tied him to the stable rack.

Thus, blind rage makes many people wreak vengeance on their enemies, thereby throwing themselves under the yoke of other people's power.

126
The Gnat and the Lion

gnat came to the lion and said, 'I am not afraid of you and you are not more powerful than me. You don't agree? Well, what kind of power do you have? The fact that you can scratch with your claws and bite with your teeth? That's the sort of thing even a woman can do when she is arguing with her husband! I am, in fact, far stronger than you are. If you agree, let's go and fight it out.' The gnat sounded his trumpet and then attacked, biting the lion around the nose where his face was not covered with hair. The lion could only wear himself out with his claws, until he finally admitted defeat. Having emerged victorious in this battle with the lion, the gnat sounded his trumpet and sang his victory ode. He then flew away—only to get entangled in the web of a spider. As he was being eaten by the spider, the gnat bitterly lamented the fact that while he had done battle with the high and mighty, he was about to be killed by such an insignificant creature.

Pride over a success should not throw us off our guard. The least of our enemies is often the most to be feared.

127

The Woodcutter and the Oak

The woodcutter cut down a mountain oak and split it in pieces, making wedges of its own branches for dividing the trunk. The oak said with a sigh, 'I do not care about the blows of the axe aimed at my roots, but I do grieve at being torn in pieces by these wedges made from my own branches.'

Misfortunes springing from ourselves are the hardest to bear.

The Fir-Tree and the Bramble

A fir-tree said boastingly to the bramble, 'You are useful for nothing at all; while I am everywhere used for roofs and houses.' The bramble answered, 'You poor creature, if you would only call to mind the axes and saws which are about to hew you down, you would have reason to wish that you had grown up a bramble, not a fir-tree.'

Better poverty without a care than wealth with its many obligations.

129

The Man and the Lion

A man and a lion were travelling along together one day when they began to argue about which of them was stronger. Just then they passed a stone statue representing a man strangling a lion.' There, you see, we are stronger than you,' said the man, pointing it out to the lion. But the lion smiled and replied, 'If lions could make statues, you would see plenty of men under the paws of lions.'

We can easily represent things as we wish them to be. It all depends on the point of view, and who tells the story.

The Dog and the Oyster

A dog, used to eating eggs, saw an oyster and, opening his mouth to its widest extent, swallowed it down with the utmost relish, supposing it to be an egg. Soon afterwards suffering great pain in his stomach, he said, 'I deserve all this torment, for my folly in thinking that everything round must be an egg.'

They who act without sufficient thought, will often fall into unsuspected danger.

131

The Dog, the Fox and the Rooster

A dog and a rooster had become friends and were making a journey together. When night fell, they came to a place in the woods. The rooster took his seat up in the branches of a tree while the dog went to sleep in a hollow at the foot of the tree. The night passed and day was dawning when the rooster crowed loudly, as roosters usually do. A fox heard the rooster and wanted to make a meal of him, so she came running up and stood at the foot of the tree and shouted to the rooster, 'You are an excellent bird and so useful to people! Why don't you come down and we'll sing some songs together, delighting in one another's company.' The rooster replied, 'Go over to the foot of the tree, my dear, and tell the watchman to let you in.' When the fox went to announce herself, the dog suddenly leaped up and grabbed the fox, tearing her to pieces.

The story shows that people are the same way: if you are wise, you take up arms to save yourself whenever you run into trouble.

132
The Lark in the Snare

A lark fell into a snare and sang a lament, 'Woe is me, wretched and unlucky bird that I am! I have brought about my own demise not for gold or silver or some object of value, but merely for a tiny bit of food.'

The story shows that people are willing to risk their lives for the sake of some petty profit.

The Wolf and the Dog

A gaunt wolf saw a huge dog wearing a large wooden restraining-collar and asked him, 'Who has chained you up and fed you like that?' 'A hunter,' replied the dog. 'Ah, God preserve wolves from him, as much as from hunger and a heavy restraining-collar!'

Better starve free than be a fat slave.

134
The Ass and the Dog

An ass and a dog were taking the same route when they found a sealed document on the ground. The ass picked it up, broke the seal, and opened it, read it aloud and the dog listened. It was all about fodder—that is to say hay, barley and straw. The dog became bored by this recital from the ass and said, 'Skip a few lines, friend. Maybe you'll come across something in there about meat and bones.' The ass scanned the rest of the document and found nothing that was of interest to the dog, who then spoke up again, 'Throw the paper away. It's completely useless.'

The story shows that different people are interested in different things.

The Lion, the Wolf and the Fox

A very old lion lay ill in his cave. All the animals came to pay their respects to their king except for the fox. The wolf, sensing an opportunity, accused the fox in front of the lion, 'The fox has no respect for you or your rule. That's why he hasn't even come to visit you.' Just as the wolf was saying this, the fox arrived, and he overheard these words. Then the lion roared in rage at him, but the fox managed to say in his own defense, 'And who, of all those who have gathered here, has rendered Your Majesty as much service as I have done? For I have travelled far and wide asking physicians for a remedy for your illness, and I have found one.' The lion demanded to know at once what cure he had found, and the fox said, 'It is necessary for you to flay a wolf alive, and then take his skin and wrap it around you while it is still warm.' The wolf was ordered to be taken away immediately and flayed alive. As he was carried off, the fox turned to him with a smile and said, 'You should have spoken well of me to His Majesty rather than ill.'

This fable shows that if you speak ill of someone, you yourself will fall into a trap.

136
The Ethiopian

A man once bought an Ethiopian slave, who had a black skin like all Ethiopians; but his new master thought his colour was due to his former owner's having neglected him, and that all he wanted was a good scrubbing. So he set to work with plenty of soap and water, and rubbed away at him with a will, but all to no purpose: his skin remained as black as ever, while the poor wretch all but died from the cold he caught.

What's bred in the bone will stick to the flesh.

The Woman and Her Drunken Husband

There was a woman whose husband was always drunk, so she came up with a plan to cure him of his drinking problem. After he had passed out one night and was sleeping the sleep of the dead, she picked him up and carried him on her shoulders to the common cemetery. Then she put him down on the ground and left him there. She waited until he had time to sober up, then she went and knocked at the entrance to the cemetery. Her husband shouted, 'Who's there?' She answered, 'I am the one who brings food to the dead.' Her husband shouted back, 'I don't want anything to eat, but bring me something to drink, my good man! It pains me to hear you speaking of food but saying nothing about a drink!' The woman then beat her breast and exclaimed, 'Woe is me! My ingenuity has not accomplished anything! O my husband, you have not simply failed to learn your lesson: you are actually even worse than before. Your problem has turned out to be permanent!'

This fable shows that people should not regularly engage in bad behaviour because at a certain point the habit will impose itself permanently, even if they do not want that to happen.

138
The Goat and the Donkey

There was a man who kept a goat and a donkey. The goat was jealous of the donkey because he was given more to eat, so she made a deceptive proposal to the donkey, under the guise of giving him advice. 'Look,' said the goat, 'you are always being punished, constantly having to turn the millstone or carry burdens on your back. Why don't you pretend to have a seizure and throw yourself into a ditch?' The donkey trusted the goat and did what she told him to do. As a result of the fall, the donkey was badly scraped and bruised. The donkey's owner summoned a doctor to recommend a remedy. The doctor said that the donkey could be cured by a potion made from the lungs of a goat. So they slaughtered the unfortunate goat, who was thus trapped in her own snare while the donkey was saved.

People who lay traps for others bring about their own destruction.

The Goatherd and the Goat

A goat strayed away from the flock, tempted by a patch of clover. The goatherd tried to call it back, but in vain. It would not obey him. Then he picked up a stone and threw it, breaking the goat's horn. The goatherd was frightened. 'Do not tell the master,' he begged the goat. 'No,' said the goat, 'that broken horn can speak for itself!'

Wicked deeds will not stay hid.

140
The Man and the Fox

There was a man who had a grudge against a fox, for the fox had caused him some damage. He managed to seize it, and in order to take his full revenge, he tied a rope which had been dipped in oil to his tail. He set fire to the rope and left him go. But, prompted by some god, the fox ran into the man's fields and set fire to all of his crops, as it was harvest time. The man ran after him helplessly, lamenting his lost crops.

One must be lenient and not allow oneself to be carried away uncontrollably, for it often happens that people easily angered cause even greater harm to themselves than to those they wish to injure and therefore increase the problems they had already.

The Sun and the Frogs

It was summer, and people were celebrating the wedding feast of the sun. All the animals were rejoicing at the event, and only the frogs were left to join in the gaiety. But a protesting frog called out, 'Fools! How can you rejoice? The sun dries out all the marshland. If he takes a wife and has a child similar to himself, imagine how much more we would suffer!'

Plenty of empty-headed people are jubilant about things which they have no cause to celebrate.

142

The Eagle and the Farmer

An eagle was caught by a farmer but the farmer let him go when he realised what he had caught. The eagle did not forget this good deed, and when he saw the farmer sitting under a wall that was on the verge of collapsing, he snatched the bandana from the man's head, wanting to rouse the man from his seat and make him stand up. After the man set off in pursuit, the kindly eagle dropped what he had snatched and thus fully repaid the man's good deed: the man would have been crushed by the wall's collapse if he had stayed there any longer. After a while the man came back to where he had been sitting and found that the upright section of the wall had fallen to the ground.

This fable shows that if anyone does you a favour you must repay them in kind.

The Heifer and the Ox

A heifer saw an ox hard at work harnessed to a plow, and tormented him with reflections on his unhappy fate in being compelled to labour. Shortly afterward, at the harvest home, the owner released the ox from his yoke, but bound the heifer with cords, and led her away to the altar to be slain in honour of the festival. The ox saw what was being done, and said to the heifer, 'For this you were allowed to live in idleness, because you were presently to be sacrificed.'

The lives of the idle can best be sacrificed.

144
The Cook and the Dog

Someone was hosting a splendid feast in the city after having performed a sacrifice. A dog belonging to the host ran into another man's dog who was a friend of his and invited him to come to the feast. The other dog came but the cook grabbed him by the leg and threw him out over the wall and into the street. When some other dogs asked him how the party had gone, the dog answered, 'Couldn't have been better! I can't even quite tell how I made my exit.'

Be shy of favours bestowed at the expense of others.

145
The Crane and the Peacock

The peacock kept waving his golden feathers back and forth while he argued with the grey-winged crane. The crane finally exclaimed, 'You may make fun of the colour of my wings, but I can rise on them up to the stars and high into the sky. You, on the other hand, can only flap those gilded feathers of yours down there on the ground, just like a rooster. You are never seen soaring up high in the sky!'

The useful is of much more importance and value, than the ornamental. I would prefer to be admired while dressed in my well-worn clothes than to live without honour, no matter how fine my clothes might be.

146
The Dog With a Bell

There was once a dog who used to snap at people and bite them without any provocation, and who was a great nuisance to every one who came to his master's house. So his master fastened a bell round his neck to warn people of his presence. The dog was very proud of the bell, and strutted about tinkling it with immense satisfaction. But an old dog came up to him and said, 'The fewer airs you give yourself the better, my friend. You don't think, do you, that your bell was given you as a reward of merit? On the contrary, it is a badge of disgrace.'

The secret spitefulness of boastful people is exposed by their vainglorious behaviour.

The Cowardly Hunter and the Woodcutter

A hunter was looking for the tracks of a lion. He asked a woodcutter if he had seen the footprints of a lion, and where the lair of the beast was. 'I will show you the lion himself,' said the woodcutter. The hunter became deathly pale with fear and, his teeth chattering, said, 'It's only the trail I'm looking for and not the actual lion.'

Some people tend to be bold in words and cowardly in deeds.

148
The Wolf and the Lion

A wolf had stolen a Lamb and was carrying it off to his lair to eat it. But his plans were very much changed when he met a lion, who, without making any excuses, took the lamb away from him. The wolf made off to a safe distance, and then said in a much injured tone, 'You have no right to take my property like that!' The lion looked back, but as the wolf was too far away to be taught a lesson without too much inconvenience, he said, 'Your property? Did you buy it, or did the shepherd make you a gift of it? Pray tell me, how did you get it?'

What is evil won is evil lost.

The Dogs and the Wolves

One day, enmity broke out between the dogs and the wolves. The dogs elected a Greek to be their general. But he was in no hurry to engage in battle, despite the violent intimidation of the wolves. 'Understand,' he said to them, 'why I deliberately put off engagement. It is because one must always take counsel before acting. The wolves, on the one hand, are all of the same race, all of the same colour. But our soldiers have very varied habits, and each one is proud of his own country. Even their colours are not uniform: some are black, some russet, and others white or ash-grey. How can I lead into battle those who are not in harmony and who are all dissimilar?'

In all armies it is unity of will and purpose which assures victory over the enemy.

150
The Fawn and the Stag

One day, a fawn said to the stag, 'Father, you are so much bigger and faster than the dogs and you have such splendid antlers to defend yourself. So why do you always run away from them?' The stag replied with a laugh, 'It's true, my child, what you say, but one thing is certain: whenever I hear the hounds baying I make a dash for it even though I don't know where I am fleeing.'

This fable shows that no amount of exhortation can reassure the faint-hearted.

151
The Lamp

Intoxicated with oil, a lamp threw out a vivid light, boasting that it was more brilliant than the sun. But a gust of wind blew up and it was extinguished instantly. Someone relit it and said, 'Light up, lamp, and be assured that the light of the stars is never eclipsed.'

You mustn't be dazzled by pride when you are held in high repute, for all that is acquired is extraneous to us.

The Country Mouse and the Town Mouse

A country mouse invited a town mouse, an intimate friend, to pay him a visit and partake of his country fare. As they were on the bare plowlands, eating there wheat-stocks and roots pulled up from the hedgerow, the town mouse said to his friend, 'You live here the life of the ants, while in my house is the horn of plenty. I am surrounded by every luxury, and if you will come with me, as I wish you would, you shall have an ample share of my dainties.'

The country mouse was easily persuaded, and returned to town with his friend. On his arrival, the town mouse placed before him bread, barley, beans, dried figs, honey, raisins, and, last of all, brought a dainty piece of cheese from a basket. The country mouse, being much delighted at the sight of such good cheer, expressed his satisfaction in warm terms and lamented his own hard fate. Just as they were beginning to eat, someone opened the door, and they both ran off squeaking, as fast as they could, to a hole so narrow that two could only find room in it by squeezing. They had scarcely begun their repast again when someone else entered to take something out of a cupboard, whereupon the two mice, more frightened than before, ran away and hid themselves. At last the country mouse, almost famished, said to his friend, 'Although you have prepared for me so dainty a feast, I must leave you to enjoy it by yourself. It is surrounded by too many dangers to please me. I prefer my bare plowlands and roots from the hedgerow, where I can live in safety, and without fear.'

It is better to live in self-sufficient poverty than to be tormented by the worries of wealth.

153
The Hare and the Fox

The hare said to the fox, 'They say you are very artful, fox. What art is it that you practice exactly?' The fox replied, 'If you don't know my arts, I will have you to dinner so that you can get a taste of my art.' The hare followed the fox to her den but the fox had nothing there to eat except for the hare himself. The hare exclaimed, 'I have learned to my cost that your name does not derive from any kind of artistry but from fraud!'

The fable shows that overly curious people often pay a very high price for recklessly indulging their curiosity.

The Wolves and the Dogs

Once upon a time the wolves said to the dogs, 'Why should we continue to be enemies any longer? You are very like us in most ways: the main difference between us is one of training only. We live a life of freedom; but you are enslaved to mankind, who beat you, and put heavy collars round your necks, and compel you to keep watch over their flocks and herds for them, and, to crown all, they give you nothing but bones to eat. Don't put up with it any longer, but hand over the flocks to us, and we will all live on the fat of the land and feast together.' The dogs allowed themselves to be persuaded by these words, and accompanied the wolves into their den. But no sooner were they well inside than the wolves set upon them and tore them to pieces.

Traitors richly deserve their fate.

155
The Donkey and the Horse

A donkey and a horse belonged to the same man, and each of them did his duty. But the horse was granted many special privileges: he had plenty of food to eat, his flowing mane was braided and decorated, and his grooms washed him down with water each and every day. The donkey, on the other hand, was always bent down under the weight of the burdens he had to carry. Then one day the horse's owner mounted him and rode off into battle. In the clash of opposing forces, the horse was wounded on more than one occasion. When the donkey saw how the horse had been degraded, he congratulated himself on his hard-working life of labour.

Better humble security than gilded danger.

The Tail and the Rest of the Body of the Snake

One day, the snake's tail developed pretensions to be the leader and led the advance. The remaining parts of the body of the snake said to it, 'How can you lead us when you have no eyes or nose like other animals?' But they could not persuade the tail, and ultimately common sense was defeated. The tail led the way, pulling blindly on the rest of the body so that in the end the snake fell into a hole full of stones and bruised her backbone and her whole body. Then the tail addressed the head, fawning and beseeching, 'Save us, please, mistress, for I was in the wrong to enter into a quarrel with you.'

This fable confounds crafty and perverse men who rebel against their masters.

157
The Rose and the Amaranth

An amaranth plant, whose flower never fades, had sprung up next to a rosebush. The amaranth said, 'What a delightful flower you are! You are desired by the gods and mortals alike. I congratulate you on your beauty and your fragrance.' The rose said, 'O amaranth, everlasting flower, I live for only a brief time and even if no one plucks me, I die, while you are able to blossom and bloom with eternal youth!'

This fable shows that it is better to last for a long time while being contented with little than to live sumptuously for a short time and then suffer a reversal of fortune, perhaps even death.

The Trumpeter

A trumpeter who summoned the assembly of troops was captured by the enemy and called out, 'Do not kill me, comrades, without due consideration and for no reason. For I have not killed any of you and apart from my brass I have nothing.' But someone replied, 'All the more reason for you to die, since, not being able to go to war yourself, you arouse everyone else to combat.'

This fable shows that those who provoke evil are the guiltier.

159
The Eagle and the Arrow

An eagle sat on a lofty rock, watching the movements of a hare whom he sought to make his prey. An archer, who saw the eagle from a place of concealment, took an accurate aim and wounded him mortally. The eagle gave one look at the arrow that had entered his heart and saw in that single glance that its feathers had been furnished by himself. 'It is a double grief to me,' he exclaimed, 'that I should perish by an arrow feathered from my own wings.'

It is bitter to be betrayed by one of your own.

The Farmer and the Tree Without Fruit

A farmer had a tree on his land that did not yield any sort of fruit whatsoever. Instead, it was a home to the sparrows and the cicadas who chirped and sang. The farmer, however, thought that the tree was useless and decided he would cut it down. He grabbed an axe and prepared to start chopping, but the cicadas and the sparrows all began to wail, shouting these words at the man, 'Listen to us, O master of the tree: we implore you to be more generous. Please do not cut down this reverend dwelling! If indeed you are resolved to do such a thing, what benefit can you possibly hope for?' The man felt no pity for the creatures and showed them no mercy as he struck the tree three times with the axe's blade. But no sooner had the man made a crack in the tree when he found there a hive of bees and honey. He took a taste and immediately dropped his axe, vowing to cherish this tree even more than his fruit-bearing trees.

This proves that, by nature, men have less love and respect for justice than a desperate eagerness for gain.

161
The Bald Knight

A bald knight, who wore a wig, went out to hunt. A sudden puff of wind blew off his hat and wig, at which a loud laugh rang forth from his companions. He pulled up his horse, and with great glee joined in the joke by saying, 'What a marvel it is that hairs which are not mine should fly from me, when they have forsaken even the man on whose head they grew.'

What Nature did not give us at birth we know we can never keep.
Naked we come, naked we depart.

The Man and the Sailors

While making a trip by sea, a certain well-to-do gentleman grew frustrated with the bad weather. As the sailors were rowing less strenuously on account of the weather, the man said to them, 'Hey you, if you don't make this ship go any faster, I will pelt you with stones!' One of the sailors then said to the man, 'I just wish we were somewhere where you could find stones to throw!'

That is how life is: we must put up with less serious losses in order to avoid worse ones.

163

The Crow and the Pitcher

A thirsty crow noticed a huge pitcher and saw that at the very bottom there was a little bit of water. For a long time the crow tried to spill the water out so that it would run over the ground and allow her to satisfy her tremendous thirst. After exerting herself for some time in vain, the crow grew frustrated and applied all her cunning with unexpected ingenuity: as she tossed little stones into the pitcher, the water rose of its own accord until she was able to take a drink.

This fable shows us that thoughtfulness is superior to brute strength, since this is the way that the crow was able to carry her task to its conclusion.

The Bird Catcher and the Cricket

A story about a bird catcher, exhorting us to pay attention to deeds, not words.

A bird catcher heard a cricket and thought he was going to make a big catch, estimating its size by the volume of its song. But when he walked up and seized his prey, he discovered that it was worthless. The bird catcher then denounced the whole process of deducing from appearances, since it often leads people to make mistaken judgments.

The fable shows that persons of no value can seem to be greater than they really are.

165
The Race Horse in the Mill

There was once a race-horse who had grown old and was sold to grind in the mill. Harnessed to the mill-stone, he ground grain all day long and into in the evening. As he was working, the old horse groaned aloud and said, 'Once I ran in the races, but now I must run in circles around this millers' course!'

Do not boast too much at the height of your powers; people often spend their old age worn out with toil and trouble.

166
The Three Bulls and the Lion

Three bulls for a long time pastured together. A lion lay in ambush in the hope of making them his prey, but was afraid to attack them while they kept together. Having at last by guileful speeches succeeded in separating them, he attacked them without fear as they fed alone, and feasted on them one by one at his own leisure.

United we stand, divided we fall.

167
The Lion and the Fox

A fox entered into partnership with a lion on the pretense of becoming his servant. Each undertook his proper duty in accordance with his own nature and powers. The fox discovered and pointed out the prey; the lion sprang on it and seized it. The fox soon became jealous of the lion carrying off the lion's share, and said that he would no longer find out the prey, but would capture it on his own account. The next day he attempted to snatch a lamb from the fold, but he himself fell prey to the huntsmen and hounds.

Keep to your place, if you would succeed.

The Olive-Tree and the Fig-Tree

The olive-tree ridiculed the fig-tree because, while she was green all the year round, the fig-tree changed its leaves with the seasons. A shower of snow fell upon them, and, finding the olive full of foliage, it settled upon its branches and broke them down with its weight, at once despoiling it of its beauty and killing the tree. But finding the fig-tree denuded of leaves, the snow fell through to the ground, and did not injure it at all.

The fable shows that people who boast of their wealth or their fortune can meet with unexpected disaster.

169

The Shepherd and the Honeybees

A story about honeybees and a shepherd, urging us not to set our hearts on wicked gains.

Some honeybees were making honey in the hollow of an oak tree. A shepherd discovered the bees' work and attempted to carry away some of the honey. The honeybees flew all around him, stinging the man with their stings. In the end the shepherd exclaimed, 'I give up! I don't need the honey if it means dealing with the bees.'

Trouble awaits you if you pursue ill-gotten gains.

The Eagle, the Snake and the Farmer

A story about an eagle and a snake, exhorting us to be the first to grant a favour.

A snake and an eagle were grappling with one another as they fought. The snake had tightened his hold on the eagle when a farmer saw them and freed the eagle from the grip of the snake. The snake was angry about what had happened, so he went and poisoned the man's drinking water. But just as the unsuspecting farmer was about to take a drink, the eagle flew down and snatched the cup out of his hands.

The man who treats others well is rewarded by gratitude.

171
The Raven and the Swan

A story about a raven, exhorting us to do what is natural to us.

The raven saw the swan and envied his beautiful white plumage. Thinking that his own colour was due to the water in which he bathed, the raven abandoned the altars where he picked up his living and instead joined the swans in the lakes and pools. This did nothing at all to change the raven's colour, but he starved to death from a lack of food.

A change of habit will not alter nature.

The Rivers and the Sea

The rivers joined together to complain to the sea, saying, 'Why is it that when we flow into your tides so potable and sweet, you work in us such a change, and make us salty and unfit to drink?' The sea, perceiving that they intended to throw the blame on him, said, 'Pray cease to flow into me, and then you will not be made briny.'

This fable depicts people who criticise someone inappropriately even though that person is actually helping them.

173

The Bull, the Lioness and the Wild Boar

A bull found a lion lying asleep and gored him with his horns until he was dead. The lion's mother showed up and wept bitterly over her son. When the wild boar saw the mother lion lamenting, he stood at a safe distance and said, 'Oh, how many people are also weeping at this very moment because their sons have been killed by you lions!'

This fable shows that what you have done to others will likewise be done to you, according to the same measure.

174
The Dogs and the Fox

Some dogs found a lion's skin and were furiously tearing it with their teeth, when a fox saw them and said, 'If that were a live lion, he would have made you feel how much sharper his claws are than your teeth.'

It is easy to kick a man that is down. This fable is for people who attack a man of renown when he has fallen from his position of power and glory.

175
The Sick Stag

A sick stag lay down in a quiet corner of its pasture-ground. His companions came in great numbers to inquire after his health, and each one helped himself to a share of the food which had been placed for his use; so that he died, not from his sickness, but from the failure of the means of living.

Evil companions bring more hurt than profit.

The Wild Ass and the Pack Ass

A wild ass saw a pack ass jogging along under a heavy load, and taunted him with the condition of slavery in which he lived, in these words, 'What a vile lot is yours compared with mine! I am free as the air, and never do a stroke of work; and, as for fodder, I have only to go to the hills and there I find far more than enough for my needs. But you! you depend on your master for food, and he makes you carry heavy loads every day and beats you unmercifully.' At that moment a lion appeared on the scene, and made no attempt to molest the pack ass owing to the presence of the driver; but he fell upon the wild ass, who had no one to protect him, and without more ado made a meal of him.

It is no use being your own master unless you can stand up for yourself.

177

The Dog Chasing a Wolf

A dog was chasing a wolf, and as he ran he thought what a fine fellow he was, and what strong legs he had, and how quickly they covered the ground. 'Now, there's this wolf,' he said to himself, 'what a poor creature he is: he's no match for me, and he knows it and so he runs away.' But the wolf looked round just then and said, 'Don't you imagine I'm running away from you, my friend: it's your master behind I'm afraid of.'

The fable shows that you should not take pride in the good qualities that actually belong to someone else.

The Man, the Mare and the Foal

A man was riding a pregnant mare and she gave birth to her foal while they were still on the road. The new-born foal followed directly behind his mother but soon became unsteady on his feet. The foal then said to the man, 'Look, you can see that I am very small and not strong enough to travel. If you leave me here, I am sure to die. But if you carry me away from here back to your home and bring me up, then later on, when I am grown, I shall let you ride me.'

The fable shows that we should do favours for someone who can do us a good deed in return.

179
The Man and the Cyclops

There was a man who was prudent in his prosperity, although he was somewhat too proud of himself. He enjoyed a comfortable life, together with his children, but after a while he lost all his money. Suffering from spiritual distress, the man uttered blasphemies and even felt compelled to commit suicide, because he would rather die than live in such wretched circumstances. Accordingly, he took his sword and set out to find a deserted place. On his way, he came across a deep pit in which he found some gold—and a great sum of gold it was! The gold had been left there by a Cyclops, which is a kind of anti-social giant. When this god-fearing man noticed the gold, he was overwhelmed at first by both terror and delight. He then cast aside his sword, took up the gold, and went back home to his children, filled with joy. Later, the Cyclops came back to the pit. When he did not find his gold there, but saw instead a sword lying in its place, he immediately picked up the sword and killed himself.

The story shows that bad things naturally happen to bad people, while good things lie in wait for people who are honest and reasonable.

The Hunetr and the Horseman

There was a hunter who had caught a hare and was carrying it home. As he went along his way, he met a man on horseback who asked him for the hare, pretending that he wanted to buy it. As soon as he got the hare from the hunter, the horseman immediately took off at a gallop. The hunter began to pursue the horseman thinking that he might catch up with him. When the horseman finally disappeared into the distance, the hunter reluctantly said, 'Go ahead then! That hare is my gift to you.'

This fable shows that people who involuntarily have their property taken from them often pretend that they made a gift of it voluntarily.

The Thief and the Innkeeper

A thief hired a room at an inn, and stayed there some days on the look-out for something to steal. No opportunity, however, presented itself, till one day, when there was a festival to be celebrated, the innkeeper appeared in a fine new coat and sat down before the door of the inn for an airing. The thief no sooner set eyes upon the coat than he longed to get possession of it. There was no business doing, so he went and took a seat by the side of the innkeeper, and began talking to him. They conversed together for some time, and then the thief suddenly yawned and howled like a wolf. The innkeeper asked him in some concern what ailed him. The thief replied, 'I will tell you about myself, sir, but first I must beg you to take charge of my clothes for me, for I intend to leave them with you. Why I have these fits of yawning I cannot tell: maybe they are sent as a punishment for my misdeeds; but, whatever the reason, the facts are that when I have yawned three times I become a ravening wolf and fly at men's throats.' As he finished speaking he yawned a second time and howled again as before. The innkeeper, believing every word he said, and terrified at the prospect of being confronted with a wolf, got up hastily and started to run indoors; but the thief caught him by the coat and tried to stop him, crying, 'Stay, sir, stay, and take charge of my clothes, or else I shall never see them again.' As he spoke he opened his mouth and began to yawn for the third time. The innkeeper, mad with the fear of being eaten by a wolf, slipped out of his coat, which remained in the other's hands, and bolted into the inn and locked the door behind him. The thief then made off with the coat and did not return again to the inn.

Every tale is not to be believed.

182
The Beetle in the Air

There was a beetle who came forth fully sated from his dung heap and saw an eagle flying high up in the air, crossing a great stretch of the sky in a brief stretch of time. The beetle then felt contempt for his own way of life and declared to his fellow beetles, 'Look at that eagle, who is so swift on the wing and so strongly built, equipped with such a savage beak and talons! If she wants, she can soar up to the clouds and plunge downwards as fast as she likes. Meanwhile, we beetles suffer from a sorry state of affairs, being not quite bugs and not quite birds. But my voice is no less pleasant than the eagle's cry, and her sheen does not outshine my own. I will not crawl around in the dung any more! From now on I will consort with the birds and fly around with them everywhere, joining their society!' The beetle then rose into the sky, emitting a song that was nothing more than a loathsome sort of buzzing. As he tried to follow the eagle into the upper air, he was unable to endure the strong winds. He fell to the ground, shaken and exhausted, far away from his home. Facing starvation, the sad beetle said, 'I don't care if they call me a bug or a bird, if only I can get back home to my dung heap!'

Disaster awaits the arrogant person who puts on airs: he will fail to get promoted and will lose his former position as well.

The Farmer, the Cattle and the Manure

A certain farmer was using his cattle to haul manure out of the stables. The cattle complained to the farmer that their labour allowed him to harvest his wheat and barley crops, supplying his household with ample food year in and year out. Therefore, said the cattle, it was hardly fair for them to have to perform the vile task of hauling manure out of the stables. The farmer then asked, 'Is it not the case that you yourselves are the source of the substance which you are now carrying away?' The cattle replied, 'Yes, that is true.' The farmer then concluded, 'So, since you are the ones who made a mess of the stable in your spare time, it is only right that you should also make some effort to clean it up!'

The same is true of grumbling, arrogant servants: they never stop reproaching their master if they have done him some good service, heedless of the rewards that have been bestowed on them, and they would like it if all of their failures were passed over in silence.

184
The Fox, the Moon and the River

A fox was out walking one night next to a river. She saw the light of the moon reflected in the water and mistook it for a piece of cheese. The fox started to lap at the water, thinking that if she could drink up all the water, she would find the cheese in the dry riverbed. The fox lapped and lapped at the water until finally she choked and died.

So every greedy man goes chasing after profit with such an intensity that he destroys himself without achieving anything.

The Goat and His Reflection

A wolf was chasing the billy goat of the herd, intending to capture him. The goat climbed up on a tall cliff where he was safe, so the wolf besieged the goat from the bottom of the cliff. After two or three days, when the wolf had grown hungry and the goat had grown thirsty, they each went away: the wolf left first in order to look for food and then the goat went away to find a drink of water. When he had quenched his thirst, the goat noticed his reflection in the water and said, 'Oh what fine legs I have and what a beautiful beard and what great horns! Just let that wolf try to make me run away: this time I will defend myself! I will not let that wolf have any power over me!' Behind the goat's back, the wolf had been listening in silence to every word the goat said. Then, as he plunged his teeth deep into the goat's flank, the wolf asked, 'What is this you are saying, brother goat?' The goat, when he realised he was trapped, said, 'O my lord wolf, I admit my mistake and beg your forgiveness! After a goat has something to drink, he says things he shouldn't. But the wolf showed no mercy and devoured the goat.

The fable warns us that weak and poor people should not try to rebel against the high and mighty.

伊索寓言

Preface to the Chinese Translation
中文譯本序

伊索寓言是世界上最古老的寓言，反映了古代希臘人對生活和自然界的看法以及人與人之間的關係。伊索寓言對世界各國影響巨大，法國的拉封丹和俄國的克雷洛夫所創作寓言中的一些動物的原型及基本情節均取材於伊索寓言。伊索被譽為"希臘寓言之父"、"西方寓言的開山鼻祖"。

伊索於公元前六世紀出生在愛琴海中的薩摩斯島上，是奴隸主雅德蒙的奴隸。他從小愛講故事，因為出眾的智慧和淵博的學識而被賜為自由民。獲得自由後，伊索經常出入小亞細亞呂底亞國王克洛伊索斯的宮廷，他的才能為國王所賞識，成為國王同希臘各城邦打交道的全權特使。在頻繁的外交活動中，他的口才得到了進一步的發揮，他講的寓言越來越受歡迎，名聲也越來越大。但是一次出使德爾斐，被誣陷偷竊聖物，慘遭當地人殺害。伊索的一生就這麼以悲劇而告終了，但他那些有着巨大生命力的寓言卻代代相傳，留存至今。在伊索離世兩百多年後，也就是公元前三世紀左右，出現了第一部他的寓言集子，其中收集了兩百多個故事，後來經不斷編訂，內容也逐漸擴充。

伊索寓言的與眾不同之處在於，主角除了一般寓言中常見的擬人化動植物之外，有很大比例是希臘神話人物，如愛神阿佛洛狄忒、主神宙斯、太陽神阿波羅等等。即使是動植物，也不全是狼和羊、獅子和狐狸、橡樹和蘆葦之類人們耳熟能詳的形象，而是採用了讀者比較陌生的甲蟲、銀鼠、河狸、螽斯、芥菜、刺李等一百多種形象，通過它們的言論、舉止、性格來刻畫人生，這使寓言的內容更加豐富，讀來頗有新鮮感。此外，大多數寓言的開頭或結尾都有一句充滿哲理的箴言來概括其深刻含義，以警世醒人。

在伊索寓言裏我們可以看到豐富的主題和深刻的寓意。將近三十篇寓言提醒人們：世上存在着邪惡。寓言的中心人物是壞人，他們為所欲為，不斷給人類製造災難，對於這種人我們只能遠遠避開。有一篇寓言講述了這樣一個故事：銀鼠愛上了一個英俊的小夥子，求愛神把它變成一個女人，但當它成了一個美麗的少女，跟着小夥子回家去以後，並未改變動物的本性，見到老鼠便"忘記了她在哪裏，她現在是誰，從牀上一下子朝老鼠撲去，想把它吃掉⋯⋯"（《銀鼠和阿佛洛狄忒》）這說明壞人的本性是改變不了的，即使改變也只是表面上收斂，一有風吹草動，他們的惡習就會暴露無遺，這也證明了一個人變壞容易變好難的道理。

命運變化莫測是伊索寓言的另一個主題。有一篇寓言說的是，有幾個人乘船去遠航，途中遭遇狂風惡浪，眼看大船就要沉沒，航海者痛哭流涕，向眾神禱告。可是等到風暴停息，躲過災難之後，他們興高采烈，擺酒慶賀，然而，正如舵手對他們說的："高興的時候我們也應該記住，風暴隨時都會再次襲來！"（見《航海者》）寓言提醒人們，命運隨時都會發生變化，人要善於適應環境，應該做到得意不要忘形，失意不要灰心。

伊索寓言還告誡人們，要善於識破欺騙的假像，有三十篇左右的寓言反映的是這個主題。比如鹿對自己頭上大而多杈的犄角十分滿意，卻對自己瘦弱的腿始終不滿意；可是當一頭獅子來襲時，它認為沒用的腿卻救了自己，而寄予希望的角卻讓樹枝纏住，因而無法繼續奔跑，獅子一下就逮住了它（見《鹿和獅子》）所以說，絕不能被假像所迷惑，寄予希望的東西往往會致人於死命，不屑一顧的東西卻常常能救人一命；花言巧語背後往往潛伏着不祥；乍看是龐然大物，常常一文不值；吹噓能創造奇跡的人，有時候連最簡單的事情都做不成。因此，要善於識破戴假面具的壞人，遠離表裏不一的偽君子。

貪慾是有害的，會使人鬼迷心竅，無法識破事情的假像——這是伊索寓言的第四個主題。最有害的是貪財，會使人失去理智，丟掉到手的東西，去追求得不到的東西；其次是虛偽、好色、嫉妒、輕信等等。在《狗和一塊肉》這篇寓言裏我們可以看到一條貪得無厭的狗：狗嘴裏叼着一塊肉過河，它在水中看到了自己的倒影，斷定這是另一條狗叼着一塊更大的肉，於是它扔掉自己嘴裏的肉，撲過去搶奪另一條狗的肉。結果它既丟了原先那塊肉，自然也沒得到另一塊肉。如果這條狗不是貪得無厭，覬覦水中倒映着的那塊根本不存在的肉，也就不會失去原來嘴裏的那塊肉。由此而引出伊索寓言的第五個主題——擺脫貪慾，人最終就會明白生活中最美好的就是知足常樂，不要去追求命中注定沒有的東西。這個主題還包括一些生活準則，例如自己的事情只能依靠自己，依靠自己的努力；選擇朋友和幫手千萬要謹慎，對朋友要知恩圖報；要學會忍受生活中的艱難，善於從錯誤中吸取教訓。

由此可見，伊索寓言的主題思想都是在總結生活經驗後得出的教人待人處事的道理，某些道理至今依然適用。比如我們從伊索寓言中可以悟出：在競爭激烈的商品經濟社會中做人要更正直、善良、知足、廉潔。

此外，有一部分寓言對下層貧民和奴隸寄予了深深的同情，在伊索筆下人物的身上，叛逆精神得到了充分的體現，而統治階級的殘暴面目也暴露無遺。

值得注意的是，伊索寓言中還有許多孿生寓言，它們題材相同，主人公卻不同，比如有兩篇寓言分別說的是：翠鳥害怕陸地上有危險，在海邊找到了避難所，誰知道這裏比陸地更危險；鹿對陸地時刻防備着，怕那兒會出現災難，而把大海當作避難所，誰知道大海卻要危險得多。即使是同一個主人公，在不同的寓言中，因為性格不同，故事情節也不同。同樣一隻螞蟻，在一篇寓言中是聰明的，在另一篇寓言中卻是愚蠢的。同樣的烏龜在兩篇寓言中也是截然不同的。

伊索寓言的語言簡潔明快，通俗易懂，形式短小精悍，形象生動逼真，風格多種多樣，更容易為現代人所接受。當然，由於時代的烙印，伊索寓言中不免存在一些消極的東西，例如在強調命運多變，要滿足現狀的同時也宣揚了"宿命論"的思想；但基本上還是一本積極向上、富有教益的故事集。

如果說拉封丹的寓言體現了法蘭西人民的樸實，克雷洛夫的寓言反映了俄羅斯人民"既有智慧又快樂的狡猾"，那麼伊索寓言表現的則是希臘精神：希臘人對整體感、個人完善和享受生活樂趣的熱愛，德爾斐的阿波羅神廟內鑴刻的兩條警句"自知"、"節制”就是此一精神的概括。伊索寓言是當時的產物，反映了當時的國家和土地上大多數人生活的精神面貌，歌頌了真善美，斥責了假惡醜，向讀者傳授了生活的真諦，具有深刻的現實意義，無論就思想性還是藝術性來說，它們對後世寓言發展的影響是非常深遠的。今天，伊索寓言早已經家喻戶曉，常被用來闡述人生道理，不僅深受廣大少年兒童的喜愛，也是成年人茶餘飯後閱讀的經典之作。

吳健平

二〇〇七年二月

1
老雕和狐狸

老雕和狐狸打算交朋友，兩人說好住在一起做鄰居，讓彼此的友誼日日加深。老雕把自己的巢築在高高的樹上，狐狸在樹下的灌木叢裏生兒育女。有一天，狐狸媽媽出去覓食，老雕肚子餓了，就撲到灌木叢裏，逮了幾隻小狐狸，回去和自己的孩子們一起飽餐一頓。狐狸回到家裏，知道出了事，心裏十分難過。它難過不光是因為孩子們死了，而是因為自己沒有辦法報復老雕：地上的走獸抓不住天上的飛禽。狐狸只好遠遠地望着樹上，咒罵這個背信棄義的傢伙。孤立無援、無可奈何的弱者又能有甚麼辦法呢？可是沒多久，老雕就不得不為自己破壞友誼的行為付出代價。有人在田裏拿一隻山羊做祭品；老雕撲向祭壇，叼走了滾燙的山羊內臟。它剛把祭品叼回巢裏，忽然一陣狂風颳來，樹上的細枝枯葉頓時燃起了熊熊大火，燒傷的雛雕紛紛掉到地上——它們還不會飛行。這時候狐狸跑過去，當着老雕的面把所有雛雕都吃了個精光。

這則寓言說明：背叛友誼的人雖然能逃脫受欺負者的報復，但終究難逃上帝的懲罰。

老雕、寒鴉和牧羊人

老雕從高高的懸崖上撲下來，抓走了羊羣裏的一隻小羊羔。寒鴉看到後非常眼饞，想要效仿老雕的行為。它大喊一聲，撲向一隻公羊。不料它的爪子被羊毛纏住，再也飛不起來，只好拼命拍打翅膀。牧羊人猜到是怎麼一回事，立刻趕來抓住了寒鴉。他剪掉了寒鴉的翅膀，晚上帶回家給孩子們玩。孩子們問，這是甚麼鳥，牧羊人答道："這是一隻寒鴉，可它自以為是一隻老雕。"

和強者、高手競爭毫無意義，失敗只會引起嘲笑。

3

老雕和甲蟲

老雕在追逐一隻兔子，兔子眼看自己無路可逃，便向它遇到的唯一過路者——一隻小小的甲蟲求助。甲蟲一面為兔子打氣，一面懇求面前的猛禽不要傷害求助於它的兔子。老雕根本不把微不足道的求情者放在眼裏，一口就吃掉了兔子。然而甲蟲對這次委屈一直耿耿於懷，它從早到晚不停監視着老雕的巢穴，每當老雕生下一隻蛋，它就爬到樹上，推蛋下來，弄碎。最後老雕到處不得安寧，便去求助宙斯，求主神撥一塊安全地方讓它生蛋，宙斯讓老雕把生下的蛋放在他的懷裏。甲蟲看到後，就把吃下肚裏的大糞滾成球，一下飛到宙斯跟前，將糞球扔到宙斯懷裏。宙斯只好站起來，抖落糞球，無意中把老雕的蛋掉在地上。聽說，從此以後老雕再也不把巢穴築在甲蟲出沒的地方了。

這則寓言告誡人們：不能小看任何人，因為任何人都不會無能到受了侮辱也不報復的地步。

夜鶯和蒼鷹

在一棵高高的橡樹上，有一隻夜鶯正放聲歌唱。肚子空空的蒼鷹看到後，撲過來逮住了它。夜鶯預感到末日來臨，便央求蒼鷹放了它。夜鶯説自己還太小，填不飽蒼鷹的肚子，要是蒼鷹沒東西可吃，可以去抓大一點的鳥。蒼鷹反駁道："要是我丟下到手的獵物，卻去追逐沒見到的獵物，那豈不成了瘋子。"

這則寓言説明，指望得到更多而拋棄到手的東西的人是天下頭號傻瓜。

5
牧羊人和野山羊

牧羊人把自己的羊羣趕到牧場，看到它們和野山羊在一起吃草，到了晚上，他把所有的羊全都趕進自己住的山洞裏。第二天天氣陰沉，他不能像往常那樣把羊趕到草地上去，只好在山洞裏照顧它們。他給自己飼養的羊一小堆草，只求不餓死它們，可是給那些野山羊一大堆草，想讓野山羊服服貼貼聽他管束。等到天氣變好以後，他又把羊羣趕到牧場去，野山羊紛紛奔向山裏，離他而去。牧羊人責罵它們忘恩負義：我照顧你們簡直無微不至，可是你們卻離我而去，無情無義。野山羊轉過身來說："我們之所以小心提防你，是因為我們昨天才剛到你那裏，但你對我們的照顧比自己原先的山羊更周到，可見，如果又有其他山羊到你那裏去，你一定會優待新來的，冷待我們。"

這則寓言說明：不能同喜新厭舊的人結交，因為他有了新朋友之後，就會冷落舊朋友。

貓和鳥

貓聽說鳥舍裏的鳥全都病倒了，便裝扮成醫生，帶上醫療儀器，來到鳥舍。它站在門旁問裏頭的鳥兒們覺得身體怎麼樣。鳥兒們回答："好得很，只要你離我們遠點。"

人類也是如此，即使刻意喬裝打扮，聰明人依舊能夠辨別壞人。

7
狐狸和山羊

狐狸掉進了一口井，無可奈何地留在那裏，因為爬不上來。一隻山羊想喝水，來到了井邊，發現井裏有一隻狐狸，便問它井裏的水好喝不好喝。狐狸很高興交上了好運，開始大肆讚美井水：“這裏的井水真是太好喝了！”並叫山羊到井下去，山羊只想到解渴，毫不猶豫地跳到井裏。山羊喝夠了水，開始和狐狸一起商量如何爬出井。這時候狐狸説，它有一個好主意，可以使它們兩個都得救：“你用前肢頂住井壁，並且低下犄角，我踩着你的背往上跳，然後再把你拉上去。”山羊樂意地採納了狐狸的建議。狐狸跳到山羊的骶骨上，撑住犄角，踩它的背一下就跑到了井口。它一爬出井，拔腿便跑掉了。山羊開始痛罵狐狸，説它破壞了它們的約定；而狐狸轉過身來説道：“唉，你呀！若是你腦袋裏的智慧和下巴上的鬍子一樣多的話，那麼你下井以前就該想好，下去後如何爬上來。”

所以説，聰明人總是三思而後行。

狐狸和獅子

狐狸生平裏從未見過獅子，有一天偶然與獅子相遇，第一次看到獅子，它嚇得魂不附體；第二次相遇，它還是感到害怕，不過沒有第一次那麼厲害；第三次再見到，狐狸便鼓起勇氣，走過去跟獅子交談了。

這則寓言說明：即使面對可怕的東西也是能夠逐漸習慣的。

9
狐狸和雪豹

狐狸同雪豹爭論誰漂亮。雪豹百般誇耀自己身上花斑點點的皮毛；狐狸聽了說道："我可比你漂亮多了，因為我雖然身上沒有花斑，但頭腦裏卻充滿各種靈巧的心思。"

這則寓言說明：靈敏的頭腦勝於美麗的身體。

10
漁夫和石頭

漁夫們拉着魚網，網沉甸甸的，眼看豐收在望，他們興高采烈，雀躍歡呼。可是等到魚網拉上來之後大家才發現，原來網裏捕到的魚並不多，裏面盡是些石頭和沙子。漁夫們心裏非常難過：遺憾的倒不是失敗本身，而是希望落了空。不過其中有個老人說道："夥伴們，別難過了，我覺得幸運和不幸是一對姐妹，有多少快樂就會有多少痛苦。"

我們也應該這樣對待生活的變幻莫測，不要一味陶醉於取得的成績，以為成績永遠屬於自己。豔陽天過後還是可能陰雨連綿。

11

狐狸和猴子

狐狸和猴子一起在路上走，彼此爭論着誰的門第高貴。雙方都費盡口舌，自吹自擂。突然，它們看到一片古墓，猴子看着這些墓，唉聲歎氣起來。"怎麼啦？"狐狸問，猴子指着墓碑感慨地説："叫我怎麼能不傷心呢！你可知道這裏面躺着的可都是我的祖先啊！它們過去都是名聲響叮噹的大人物呢！"可是狐狸針鋒相對地説："吹你的牛去吧，隨你怎麼吹都行，因為他們當中沒有一個人會死而復生，揭穿你的謊言。"

人類中的撒謊者同樣如此，他們專挑死無對證的事吹牛。

狐狸和葡萄

飢餓的狐狸看見葡萄架上掛着一串串成熟的葡萄，饞涎欲滴。它很想摘葡萄，可是夠不到，無可奈何，只好走開，嘴裏自言自語地說道："葡萄是酸的！"

有些人同樣如此，他們無法獲得成功是因為自己無能，卻總是怪罪於客觀因素。

13
貓和公雞

貓捉到一隻公雞，想找個冠冕堂皇的藉口把它吃掉。起先它指責公雞半夜啼鳴，驚擾了人們，使大家睡不踏實。公雞辯解道，它這樣做對人類是有益的，它喚醒大家去工作。於是貓又說：“不過你仍然是有罪的；你違背倫理道德，同自己的母親和姐妹交配。”公雞又辯解道，它這樣做對主人是有利的，它竭盡全力，為的是讓主人得到更多的雞蛋。這下貓倉皇失措地喊道：“那麼你認為，因為你做甚麼事都有理由，我就不該吃你了嗎？”它吃了公雞。

這則寓言説明：壞人行兇作惡總是明目張膽，我行我素，用不着找冠冕堂皇的藉口。

14
失去尾巴的狐狸

隻狐狸中了捕獸器的陷阱而失去了尾巴，它覺得活在世上很羞恥。於是，它決定慫恿其他狐狸也割掉尾巴，只要大家全都沒有尾巴，他就能掩蓋自己的缺陷。它把所有狐狸通通叫來，用花言巧語來說服它們割掉自己的尾巴，說甚麼長尾巴不漂亮，尾巴只是身上多餘的負擔，尤其是遭到敵人野狗追趕的時候；彼此想坐下來談話時也會增添麻煩。可是其中一隻較老的狐狸說："唉，你呀！若不是你自己失去了尾巴，你絕不會給我們提這個建議的。"

這則寓言針對那些為了一己私利，並非真心為親朋好友出好主意的人。

15
狐狸和鱷魚

狐狸同鱷魚爭論誰的門第高貴。鱷魚滔滔不絕吹噓自己祖先的榮耀，最後它說自己的祖先是體操教練，狐狸對此諷刺道："你少來！看你身上的皮膚就知道，你不曉得已經幾百年沒出門曬過太陽了。"

事實總會揭穿謊言。

16
漁夫和鮪魚

漁夫們出海去捕魚，可是不管他們花了多少力氣，結果還是一無所獲，於是大家坐在船裏，垂頭喪氣。忽然一條逃命的鮪魚剛好蹦到他們的船裏，大家一把抓住魚，運到城裏，把它賣了。

運氣常常會賜給我們原先無法獲得的東西。

17
狐狸和樵夫

狐狸為了逃避獵人的追捕，拼命向前跑。它看到一位樵夫，便向他哀求，求樵夫把自己藏起來。樵夫於是讓狐狸躲進了他的小茅屋。不一會，獵人趕來了，他們問樵夫有沒有看見跑到這裏的狐狸？樵夫大聲回答說："沒看見。"可同時卻比了個手勢，指了指狐狸藏身的地方。獵人沒注意到樵夫的手勢，相信了他的話。等到獵人離開以後，狐狸跑出屋，一言不發就走了。樵夫開始數落它：我救了你一命，你卻連一句感謝的話都不說。狐狸反駁說："要是你只動口不動手，我當然會感謝你。"

這則寓言可以用來指責那些話說得漂亮，事情卻處理得很糟的人。

變胖的狐狸

隻飢腸轆轆的狐狸看見樹洞裏有牧羊人留下的麵包和肉，便迫不及待地爬進洞，把所有的東西一股腦兒全吃了。吃完東西後，它的肚子脹得鼓鼓的，沒有辦法再從洞裏爬出來，它只好唉聲歎氣，嘴裏直哼哼。另一隻狐狸從旁邊經過，聽到了它的呻吟，走過來問出了甚麼事。當了解了事情真相後便說道："你只好乖乖地留在這裏，直到你變回原來的樣子，到時候再爬出來就不費力氣了。"

這則寓言說明：困境會隨着時間的推移自然而然地消逝。

19
翠鳥與海

翠鳥是一種喜歡離羣索居、終年生活在海上的小鳥。相傳翠鳥為了躲避獵人，往往會在海岸邊的岩礁上安家築巢。每當它要下蛋時，就會飛到海岬上找個懸崖峭壁築巢。有一天，翠鳥外出覓食，忽然狂風大作、波濤洶湧，海水沖毀了鳥巢，所有的小翠鳥都溺水身亡。翠鳥媽媽回到家裏，目睹了一切經過，大聲喊道：＂我真不幸，太不幸了！我害怕陸地上有危險，在海邊找個避難所，誰知道這裏比陸地更危險。＂

有些人同樣如此，他們對敵人處處戒備，不料卻反遭比敵人更危險、誤認是自己朋友之人的傷害。

20
漁夫

漁夫在河裏捕魚。他在河上張開大漁網，隨後用繩子拴住一塊石頭，用石頭擊起水來。他用這種辦法嚇唬魚，讓想逃命的魚意外地自投羅網。有個當地居民看到之後便責罵漁夫把水給攪渾了，使得附近居民喝不到潔淨的水。漁夫反駁道："要是我不把水攪渾，那我就只好等着餓死了！"

一個國家裏的陰謀家也是如此，就是要讓陰謀得逞並在社會上引起騷亂，他們才覺得高興。

21
狐狸和面具

狐狸溜進雕塑家的工作室，翻遍所有的東西，找到一個悲劇演員的面具，它舉起面具說道："這算甚麼腦袋，裏面連腦髓也沒有！"

這則寓言諷刺四肢發達、頭腦簡單的人。

騙子

有個窮人生了病非常難受。他向眾神許諾，要是能使他痊癒，他就拿一百頭牛來獻祭。於是眾神打算測試他，立刻讓他的病情緩解了。他從病榻上爬起來，可是他沒有真正的牛，便用脂油捏了一百頭牛的模型獻祭，嘴裏説道："噢眾神，請收下吧，收下我的諾言！"眾神們決定用欺騙來回報欺騙，他們託夢給他，讓他趕緊到海岸邊去，説在那裏可以找到一千個德拉克馬古希臘銀幣。窮人樂壞了，立刻跑去岸邊。一到了那裏馬上就落入強盜手中，強盜們把他帶走並賣給別人家當奴隸。確實有一千個德拉克馬銀幣，只不過不是給這個可憐的窮人，而是那羣強盜。

這則寓言諷刺説謊的人。

23
燒炭工人與印染工人

有位獨居的燒炭工人，生活自給自足，好不愉快。一天，附近搬來了一個印染工人，燒炭工人便向對方提議可以住在一起；這樣一來他們很快就可以彼此熟識，況且合住一間房子費用還要便宜些。可是印染工不同意：「不，這無論如何也不行。任何我漂白的東西或地方，要不了多久就會被你的碳弄髒。」

這則寓言說明不同的東西不能混在一起。

24
經歷過海難的人們

一個富有的雅典人和其他乘客在海上航行，忽然一陣狂風暴雨掀翻了船，所有的人都立刻游水逃命，只有雅典人沒完沒了地呼喊着雅典娜，發誓只要能得救，一定用無數祭品來祭奠她。這時候一個難友游到他身邊，對他說："光是嘴裏向雅典娜祈禱是不夠的，你的手腳也要動起來。"

我們不應該只是一昧地祈禱，要懂得自己照顧自己。

25
兇手

有個人犯了殺人罪,被死者的親屬到處追緝。他逃到尼羅河邊,卻碰上了一隻狼,嚇得他連忙爬到垂在河邊的一棵樹上躲藏;誰知他又看到一條蜿蜒在樹上的蛇,於是只好跳入水中,可是水裏正好有一條鱷魚張開大嘴在等着他,一口就把他吞下了肚。

這則寓言告訴我們:惡有惡報。

26
許諾不兌現的人

有個窮人生了病，覺得渾身不舒服，快要支持不住了。醫生也認為他已經回天乏術，便放棄治療了。他於是向眾神祈禱，許諾要是自己能夠康復，就獻上一百頭牛做為祭品，同時贈與厚禮。他的妻子在一旁問道："你用甚麼來兌現諾言？"他回答："難道你真以為我康復後會給眾神任何東西嗎？"

這則寓言證明了人們往往只在口頭上許諾，卻從無兌現諾言的想法。

27
人與薩堤羅斯

薩堤羅斯是希臘神話裏的森林之神，性好歡娛，耽於淫慾。傳說從前有一個人和薩堤羅斯一度成為很要好的朋友。冬天到了，天氣開始變得寒冷，這個人就把雙手放到嘴邊，開始往手上哈氣。薩堤羅斯問他為甚麼這麼做，人回答這是在嚴寒中讓手取暖的辦法。之後他們坐下一起吃飯，食物很燙，於是人就拿了一點放到嘴邊吹着。薩堤羅斯又問他這是幹甚麼。人回答因為食物太燙了需要先冷卻才能吃。於是薩堤羅斯說："不，老兄，你從同一張嘴裏既吹出熱氣，又吹出冷氣，我沒辦法和你這種人成為朋友。"

我們也應該時刻提防那些陽奉陰違的雙面人朋友，他們的友誼是不可信的。

瞎子

有個盲人光靠自己的觸覺，就能夠猜出任何一種被放到自己手中的動物。一天，有人給他一隻小狼想讓他猜。他撫摸了一下，猶豫不決地說："我不知道這是小狼還是小狐狸，我只知道：最好不要把它放到羊羣中。"

邪惡的本性想藏也藏不住。

29
占星家

有個占星家養成習慣每天晚上都會出門看星星。有一天他在郊區散步，所有的心思都集中在天上，卻不慎掉入一口水井。他又哭又喊。有個路過的人聽到哭喊聲便走了過來，馬上猜到了是怎麼一回事，便對他說道："唉！你呀！想弄清楚天上的事，卻沒有注意地上發生的事。"

這則寓言告訴我們不要好高騖遠，好好珍惜、守護身邊的人事物。

農夫和他的兒子們

有個農夫生命垂危，他希望日後自己的兒子們能繼承家業，成為最頂尖的農夫。於是他把所有人叫到身邊並對他們說："孩子們，在一根葡萄藤底下埋藏着我的財寶。"他才剛咽氣，兒子們就立刻揮起鐵鍬翻遍了家裏所有的土地。最後財寶並沒有找到，但是掘鬆了的土地卻給他們家帶來了比那筆財寶更為豐碩的收成。

這則寓言說明了勞動是人類的財富。

31
池塘內的青蛙

沼澤地乾涸以後，兩隻原先留在裏頭的青蛙便開始去尋找新的棲身之地。它們來到一口井邊，其中一隻青蛙不假思索就建議跳到井裏去。可是另一隻青蛙說道："要是這裏的水也乾了，那我們要怎麼從裏面爬出來呢？"

這則寓言告誡我們不要輕舉妄動。

32
北風和太陽

北風和太陽相互爭論誰的本事大。最後它們說定，誰能讓地上的路人脫下衣服誰就獲勝。北風開始猛烈地呼嘯起來，可是路人們卻把身上的衣服裹得緊緊的。北風只好更加猛烈地怒吼起來，而受凍的人們卻把衣服越裹越緊。最後北風累了，只好換太陽去試試。起初太陽只發出一點暖洋洋的光芒，人們開始脫去身上多餘的衣服，最後太陽火辣辣地烤起來，結果所有的人都承受不了炎熱，脫光了所有衣服，紛紛跳進附近的小河消暑。

這則寓言告訴我們：好言相勸往往比強迫有效。

33
籠中鳥和蝙蝠

有隻黃雀被關進掛在窗口的鳥籠裏，一天半夜裏它放聲歌唱。聽到歌聲，一隻蝙蝠飛了過來，它問黃雀為甚麼白天不唱歌，只在晚上唱？黃雀回答自己這麼做是有原因的：它當初就是因為在白天唱歌才被關進了鳥籠，從此以後它就變聰明了。於是蝙蝠就說："如果在沒被抓住前你有這麼小心就好了，現在一切都無濟於事了。"

一失足成千古恨。

農夫與狗

由於外面天氣過於惡劣，農夫只能困坐家中，無法出門獲取食物；最後只好先殺掉了自己飼養的一隻綿羊充飢。暴風雨繼續肆虐；他又宰了自己養的山羊當作食物。可是壞天氣依舊沒有結束的跡象。接着輪到牛羣們遭殃了。這時，兩條負責看門的狗看着主人的行動，便私底下商量："我們該逃離這個地方了；既然主人對和自己一起辛苦幹活的牛都不發善心，那就更別指望他能放過我們。"

這則寓言説明：最該提防的是那些連親人也要冒犯的人。

35
一捆樹枝

農夫的兒子們老是爭吵不休，他一次次勸他們和睦相處，但是無論説甚麼似乎都無濟於事，最後農夫決定用事實來説服他們。他叫兒子們拿一捆樹枝來，接着農夫把樹枝交給他的兒子們，讓他們試試把這些樹枝折斷。兒子們一個個嘗試，不管費多大的勁，誰也沒辦法把整捆樹枝折斷。就在這時父親拆開捆着的樹枝，抽出其中的一根交給他們，結果毫不費力就把它折斷了。於是農夫就對兒子們説道：“你們也是一樣的，我的孩子們。只要你們能和睦相處，任何敵人也無法戰勝你們；但要是你們彼此相互爭吵，那麼任何人都能輕而易舉地制服你們。”

這則寓言告訴我們：獨木難支，眾志成城。

女主人和女僕

有個勤勉的寡婦僱了好幾個女僕，每天夜裏只要雞一叫，她就催着她們起牀幹活。連續不斷的勞動使女僕們個個疲憊不堪，所以大家決定把家裏那只公雞勒死，都是因為公雞在半夜三更把女主人叫醒，才有這一切的不幸和苦難。可是等到她們把公雞勒死後，發現情況反而變得更糟。由於現在夜裏都不知道時間，這位女主人常常隨意叫醒女僕，但時間往往比以前更早。

對於許多人來說，他們自己的計謀往往會成為不幸的根源。

37
算命的女人

有個會算命的女人常常用咒語阻止眾神發怒，並以此為生，日子過得舒舒服服，也積攢了不少錢財。可是有些人指責她褻瀆神靈，於是上告當局，經過審判她被判處了死刑。看到她的下場，有個人就說了："你阻止得了眾神發怒，怎麼卻無法平息人的憤怒？"

這則寓言揭露了那些愛唱高調，事實上卻毫無本事的騙子。

老婆婆和大夫

有個老婆婆患了眼疾，所以她請來一個大夫，答應若能治好病就會付給他報酬。這個大夫每次一來就用藥膏封住老婆婆的眼睛，趁她閉着眼睛看不見的時候，順手牽羊拿走她家裏的東西。當大夫把老婆婆家裏能拿的東西全都拿走以後，治療便結束了。他向老婆婆索討她答應過的報酬，老婆婆拒絕了，於是大夫就將她拉到執政官那裏。老婆婆表示，她只答應治好病才付報酬，可自己在治療以後視力不僅沒有變好，反而變更差了。"從前我看得見自己家裏的所有東西，"老婆婆說，"可現在我甚麼也看不見。"

貪財的壞人無意中會使自己原形畢露。

39
演說家得馬特

演説家得馬特有天在所有雅典市民面前演説，可是聽眾漫不經心。於是他請求大家允許他講一個伊索的寓言，大家同意了。他就開始講："得墨忒耳、燕子和鰻鱺一起走在大街上，不知不覺來到了河邊。燕子張開翅膀飛過了河，鰻鱺縱身一躍，潛入了水中……"説到這他住口不説了。"那得墨忒耳怎麼辦呢？"大家紛紛問他。"得墨忒耳站着，對着你們發怒，"得馬特説，"因為你們只愛聽伊索的寓言，國家大事你們卻不關心。"

人類當中也有些人非常無知，對該做的事情不屑一顧，卻只熱衷於湊熱鬧。

兩個旅人和熊

兩個好朋友走在路上，忽然迎面跑來一隻熊。一個人立刻爬上樹躲了起來。另一個眼看自己逃脫不了，便往地上一躺，裝死。當熊走到他跟前聞他時，他就屏住呼吸，一動也不動，因為聽說熊不吃死人。熊走掉了，躲在樹上的人下來後問朋友，熊在他耳邊說了些甚麼？對方回答說：“熊低聲地叫我以後別再和這樣的朋友一同上路，這種人碰到危難只顧自己逃命，而不會照顧朋友。”

這則寓言說明患難才能見真情。

41
兩個旅人和一把斧頭

兩個朋友一同旅行，其中一個人發現了一把斧頭，於是便跟另一個人說："你看，我發現了一把斧頭！"但另一個朋友說："不對！不是'你'發現了斧頭，而是'我們'發現了斧頭。"沒多久他們就遇上了那位丟失了斧頭的主人，這時手裏拿着斧頭的人對身旁的朋友說："這下我們完了！"那個朋友說："你說錯了，不是'我們'完了，而是'你'完了，因為你發現斧頭的時候可沒有我的份！"

這則寓言說明，不肯與人有福同享的人，也別指望別人與你有難同當。

42
養蜂人

有個人來到養蜂場，剛好養蜂人不在，他就順手牽羊拿走了蜂房和蜂蜜。養蜂人回來後發現蜂箱空空如也，便站在蜂箱前仔細查看。這時候，蜜蜂從田野裏飛回家，看到養蜂人在蜂箱前，紛紛蜇起他來。養蜂人被蜇得疼痛難忍，就對蜜蜂說："你們這些卑鄙的東西！偷你們蜂房的人你們沒碰一下就飛走了，現在卻蜇咬為你們擔憂操心的人！"

有些人也是這樣不善於分辨敵友；對敵人不加防備，對待朋友卻像對罪犯那般冷酷。

43
鹿和獅子

一頭口渴的鹿漫步到了泉水邊。喝水時，它發現了自己在水中的倒影，便開始欣賞起自己又大又多杈的犄角來，但它對自己那兩條瘦弱的腿卻始終不滿意。正在沉思的時候，一頭獅子朝它撲來。鹿撒開腿沒命似地逃，把獅子遠遠拋在後面。要知道鹿的功夫在腿上，而獅子的功夫在心裏。當鹿在開闊地帶奔跑時，它遙遙領先，始終安然無恙，可是當它跑到小樹林裏時，自己那多杈的角就被樹枝給纏住了，無法繼續奔跑，於是獅子一下子就捉住了它。鹿預感到死期將至，自言自語地說："我真是不幸！我自認沒用的東西救了自己一命，而寄予希望的東西卻把我給毀了！"

最重要、最有價值的東西往往最被低估了。

44
航海者

有幾個人乘上大船出發遠航。當他們遠離海岸、到達大海中央時，海上忽然掀起了狂風惡浪，大船眼看就要沉沒。其中有一個人扯着身上的衣服，痛哭流涕地對着慈父般的眾神呼喚，他向眾神許諾，要是大船安然無恙，他就向他們獻上感恩的祭品。風暴終於停息了，海上再次風平浪靜。航海者出乎意料躲過了災難，大家興高采烈，擺酒設宴，又蹦又跳。然而，嚴厲的舵手以命令的口氣對他們説："不行，朋友們，高興的時候我們也應該記住，風暴隨時都會再次襲來！"

這則寓言告誡人們，不要得意忘形，要記住，命運是變化莫測的。

45
狐狸和猴子

世上所有的動物們曾經開過一次大會，由於在過程中猴子一直唱唱跳跳、逗大家開心，於是大家便選它做百獸之王。狐狸對此十分眼紅，有一天它看見一個捕獸夾裏有一塊肉，便把猴子帶到夾子前，説自己發現了這個寶物但是沒拿，想把這當作體面的禮物留給獸王。猴子輕信了狐狸的話，最後被捕獸夾給夾住了。它責罵狐狸卑鄙無恥，可是狐狸卻説："唉猴子，憑你這點智慧今後還想在眾獸面前稱王稱霸？"

有些人也是如此，因為做事輕率，最後招致失敗而成為眾人的笑柄。

兩隻甲蟲

在一個小島上生活着一頭公牛，它的糞便通常是島上兩隻甲蟲的食物。冬天來了，一隻甲蟲對它的同伴說：“我想飛到岸上去，讓你在這兒有充足的食物。我到那裏去過冬，要是找到很多食物，我就帶回來給你吃。”甲蟲飛到岸上，找到一大堆新鮮的糞便，它便留在岸邊生活了。冬天過去了，它回到了島上。同伴見它又胖又結實，就責備它沒有實現諾言。它回答說：“你該罵的不是我，而是這個大自然：因為這裏的東西只能吃，不能拿。”

這則寓言針對那些只願錦上添花、不肯雪中送炭的人。

47

下金蛋的母鵝

有個人特別崇敬赫耳墨斯這位眾神的使者、亡靈的接引神，他掌管商業、交通、畜牧、競技、演說，甚至是欺詐和盜竊。為此赫耳墨斯送給他一隻會下金蛋的母鵝，但是這個人等不及慢慢發財。他斷定鵝的肚子裏一定全都是金子，於是他毫不猶豫地把鵝宰了。結果卻大失所望，因為他在鵝的肚子裏只找到了它的內臟，但從此以後卻再也得不到金蛋了。

貪財的人往往都是這樣，貪圖大利，卻把已經擁有的東西也丟失了。

兩條狗

有個人養了兩條狗：一條訓練成獵狗，另一條在家看門。每當獵狗從野外帶回來獵物時，他總要丟一塊給看家狗吃。獵狗生氣了，開始數落看家狗。它說自己每次去打獵總是累得筋疲力盡，而看家狗甚麼活也不幹，只知道坐享其成，靠它的勞動撐飽肚子。看家狗反駁說："該罵的不是我，而是主人，因為是主人讓我養成不勞而獲，依靠別人勞動過活的習慣。"

養子不教為父母之過。

49
丈夫和妻子

有個人娶了一個脾氣古怪、誰也受不了的妻子。他打算試探一下妻子在娘家的表現和行為舉止是不是也如此。於是，他找了一個冠冕堂皇的理由，把妻子打發回娘家去了。幾天後，妻子回來了，丈夫劈頭就問，娘家人待她怎麼樣。妻子回答說："牧羊人和他的助手都不喜歡我。"丈夫說："是嗎？老婆，要是連那些一直和牲口留在一起，整天都不在家的人都對你有意見的話，那麼那些整天都跟你在一起的人們還有甚麼話可說呢！"

通過小事往往能夠看清大事，透過表象常常可以發現本質。

50
寒鴉和眾鳥

宙斯要給眾鳥選派一個國王,他定下日子,通知所有的鳥前來聚會。寒鴉知道自己長得醜陋不堪,便出去收集各種鳥的羽毛,插在身上打扮自己。聚會的日子到了,它將自己打扮得漂漂亮亮,來到宙斯面前。宙斯見它這麼美麗,正打算選它為國王;可是眾鳥卻非常憤慨地把寒鴉團團圍住,紛紛從它身上拔下屬於自己的羽毛。最後那些插上去的羽毛被拔得精光,它又再次變回了那隻普通的寒鴉。

敞開心胸接納自己,別做表裏不一的人。

51
宙斯和狐狸

宙斯對狐狸的智慧和計謀十分欣賞，便任命它為國王，統治那些無知的動物。不過宙斯同時也想知道，當命運改變以後，狐狸卑鄙的心靈是否也會發生變化？於是，當狐狸被抬着坐在轎子裏的時候，宙斯故意在它面前放了一隻金龜子。金龜子圍着轎子團團轉，最後狐狸終究忍受不了，拋開了國王的尊嚴，從轎子上跳下來捉金龜。宙斯大發雷霆，把狐狸變回了原來的樣子。

這則寓言說明：江山易改，本性難移。

螞蟻和甲蟲

炎熱的夏天，螞蟻在耕地裏東奔西跑，收集小麥和大麥，準備儲存起來過冬。甲蟲看到螞蟻這麼辛苦，對它深表同情。其他動物都舒舒服服地在休息、閒蕩，只有螞蟻在這麼炎熱的季節也不得不辛勤地勞動。螞蟻對此一言不發。冬天來了，糞肥被雨水沖掉了，甲蟲只好餓着肚子來找螞蟻，求螞蟻給它一些糧食。螞蟻對它說：“唉！甲蟲，要是我勞動那會兒，你自己也幹點活的話，現在就不至於落到忍飢挨餓的地步了。”

有備無患。

53
鮪魚和海豚

鮪魚為躲避海豚的追捕，嘩啦啦地拍打着水，向前游去。海豚眼看就要抓住它了，只見鮪魚一下蹦到岸上，海豚緊追不捨，也蹦到了岸上。鮪魚回頭一看，發現海豚已經奄奄一息，就說："既然我看到了欲置我於死地的罪魁禍首和我同歸於盡，那麼現在我死而無憾了。"

這則寓言說明：要是人們親眼見到給自己帶來不幸的罪魁禍首到頭來也落得受苦受難的下場，心裏也會好受一些。

醫生和病人

 個家庭有親屬過世了，正當家屬正忙着處理相關事宜的時
候，有位也在場的醫生對其中一位家人説：“要是他沒有喝
酒，也早點接受治療的話，就不會送命。”那人對醫生説：“老兄，
這些事情你為甚麼不早一點説呢！現在説已經無濟於事了。”

這則寓言説明：幫助朋友應該及時，當事情已無可挽回，就別再
冷言冷語。

55
捕鳥人和眼鏡蛇

捕鳥人拿起粘鳥膠和樹條出發去捕鳥，他看到一棵大樹上停着一隻鷦鴣，便打算捕捉它。他把帶去的樹條首尾相接，開始全神貫注地、機警地注視着樹上。他朝樹上看得出了神，沒發現腳下躺着一條眼鏡蛇，一不留神踩在蛇身上，蛇靈巧地閃開，猛然咬了他一口。快咽氣的時候，他自言自語地說："我真倒霉！原本想要捉鳥，沒想到自己卻先遭了難，丟了性命。"

害人往往先害己。

螃蟹和狐狸

螃蟹爬出海面，來到岸上定居。飢腸轆轆的狐狸看到後連忙跑過去，一把抓起螃蟹，想拿它來當充飢的食物。螃蟹眼看自己就要被狐狸吃掉，唉聲歎氣地說："有甚麼辦法，我活該倒霉。我本是大海的居民，卻異想天開，到陸地上來生活。"

有些人也是如此，他們放下自己的事情不做，去插手別人的事，結果一事無成，活該倒霉。

57
河狸

河狸是一種四條腿的動物，生活在池塘裏。傳說，它的睾丸可以製成某些藥品。河狸明白大家之所以要獵殺它的原因。起初，它憑着自己的四條飛毛腿拼命奔跑，指望能安然無恙地逃脫。但要真是瀕臨絕境的話，它也已經做好盤算要把自己的睾丸咬下、扔掉，以此來救自己一命。

聰明人為了挽救生命往往不惜犧牲自己的財富。

小偷和公雞

小偷潛入一間屋子，可是屋裏除了公雞，甚麼也沒有。他抓起公雞，拔腿就溜。公雞見自己被捆了起來，便央求小偷手下留情，同時表示自己是益禽，能喚醒人們去工作。可是小偷說："正因為如此我才把你捆起來，誰叫你叫醒人們，讓我無法行竊。"

這則寓言說明：凡是對好人有益的事情，往往會引起壞人的刻骨仇恨。

59
渡鴉和狐狸

渡鴉叼着一塊肉停在樹上,狐狸見了很想把肉佔為己有。它站在渡鴉面前,開始吹捧渡鴉長得又高大又美麗,絕對有資格成為鳥中之王;當然,若是還有一副好嗓子,那就一定能當上鳥王。渡鴉聽後很想炫耀一下自己的嗓子,張開叼着肉的嘴,呱呱地大聲叫起來。狐狸跑過來,撿起肉,說道:"唉,渡鴉,要是你能再更聰明一點的話,那麼你就是當之無愧的大王了。"

這則寓言用來諷刺無知的人。

寒鴉和鴿子

寒鴉看到鴿子窩裏的鴿子有很好的伙食，便在全身抹上白粉，想要跟鴿子一起生活。起初它一聲不吭，於是鴿子們把它當成自己的同類，沒有趕走它。可是當它忘乎所以、啞啞亂叫時，鴿子們立刻認出了它的聲音，一下子就把它趕走了。寒鴉沒得到鴿子的食物，只好回到自己的窩裏，可是窩裏的寒鴉見它一身白羽毛，不承認它是寒鴉，不願和它同住，也將它趕了出去。就這樣，寒鴉本想追求兩個利益，結果卻一個也沒得到。

由此可見，我們應該滿足於已經擁有的一切，要記住，貪婪不會帶來任何好處，卻有可能失去一切。

61
獵狗、獅子和狐狸

獵狗看到一頭獅子，便沖了上去。獅子回過頭來，大吼一聲，狗喪魂落魄，跑得遠遠的。狐狸看到狗就說："你的腦袋瓜子太不好使，想去追獅子，卻光是聽了它的聲音就害怕！"

這則寓言可以用來諷刺那些放肆無禮的人，他們老愛誹謗比自己強得多的人；可是只要對方一開口反駁他們，他們立刻就啞口無言。

62
狗和一塊肉

有隻狗嘴裏叼着一塊肉渡河，它在水中看到了自己的倒影。狗斷定這是另一條狗叼着一塊更大的肉，於是它扔掉自己嘴裏的肉，撲過去搶奪另一條狗的肉。結果它既失去了這塊肉，也沒得到另一塊肉。最後它一塊肉也沒得到，因為那塊肉根本就不存在，而它原有的那塊肉最後給河水沖走了。

貪婪沒有好下場。

63
狗和狼

狗在農舍前面睡覺，狼看見狗便一把抓住，想吃掉它。狗求狼這一次先放過自己。狗說："現在的我既瘦弱又乾瘪，不過我的主人馬上就要舉行婚禮，要是你現在放過我，以後就能吃到更肥的狗肉。"狼相信了狗，暫時先把狗放了。可是幾天後，等到狼再回來一看，狗正在屋頂上睡覺。狼叫狗下來，提醒它先前約定過的事，狗卻對它說："唉，老兄，要是你下次再看到我在房子前面睡覺的話，可別再推遲到婚禮以後吃我。"

不經一事，不長一智。

兔子和青蛙

　　一羣兔子意識到自己是多麼膽小無用，決定集體投水自殺。

　　它們來到池塘邊的陡岸，池塘邊的青蛙聽到兔子們的腳步聲，就紛紛跳進深水裏。見此情景，一隻兔子對其他兔子說：“我們還是別跳吧！你們瞧，世上還有比我們更膽小的動物呢！”

世上永遠會有比你還要不幸的人，所以別再自怨自艾了。

65
獅子和農夫

獅子愛上了農夫的女兒，前來向她求婚。農夫既不打算把女兒嫁給猛獸，又不敢得罪獅子。他絞盡腦汁想了個辦法。獅子依然堅持要娶農夫的女兒，農夫就說他認為獅子會是個不錯的新郎，可是要他把女兒嫁出去，得先等到獅子拔去自己的利齒，削去自己的利爪，要不然新娘會害怕的。墮入情網的獅子心甘情願地弄掉了自己的利齒和利爪，但是這樣一來農夫就不怕獅子了。當獅子再來找他時，農夫就掄起棍子把它從家裏趕跑了。

這則寓言說明，對敵人要時刻保持警惕，如果輕信對方，自動解除武裝，就會輕而易舉地成為對方的獵物。

年老的獅子

獅子上了年紀，無法靠力氣為自己弄到食物，決定用計謀來取勝。它鑽進山洞，躺在那兒佯裝生病。野獸們紛紛前來探望，它先是誇獎了大家一番，接着把它們一個個吞進肚裏。許多野獸都因此而送了命。狐狸猜中了它的計謀，雖然跑了過來，卻沒有進山洞，只是在外頭問獅子身體怎麼樣。獅子說："不舒服！"然後反問狐狸為甚麼不進洞？狐狸回答說："要是我沒有親眼目睹進洞的野獸不計其數，但卻一個也沒有出來的話，我當然會進去。"

聰明的人能夠預測兇險，也懂得躲避。

67
獅子和公牛

獅子在圈地裏看見一頭肥牛，於是暗暗盤算用計將其誘騙過來，好飽餐一頓。獅子對公牛說自己打算食用一頭綿羊，並邀請對方前來赴宴；其實獅子早就計劃好，等到公牛一就座便立刻收拾它。公牛一來就發現鍋子很多，烤肉的工具也很齊全，惟獨不見綿羊的影子。公牛二話不說，拔腿就走。獅子故意難過地責問公牛為甚麼一聲不吭就走。公牛回答說："我這麼做是有原因的，因為我發現今天要被犧牲的不是綿羊而是我。"

這則寓言說明：惡人的陰謀瞞不過聰明人。

獅子和海豚

獅子在海岸邊散步，看到浪花裏有一條海豚，便向它提議結成聯盟：我們兩個，一個是海洋動物之王，一個是大地之王，還有誰比我們更適合成為好朋友和同盟呢？海豚立刻就答應了。沒過多久，獅子和野牛發生了爭鬥，獅子大聲呼救，請求海豚助它一臂之力。海豚很想鑽出海面去幫忙，可是力不從心，獅子就責備它背叛朋友。海豚對獅子說："你該罵的不是我，而是大自然，都怪它讓我成了海洋動物，沒辦法到陸地上去。"

應該挑選能夠雪中送炭的人做朋友。

69
獅子和熊

獅子和熊捕獲了一頭小鹿，為了分贓，它們打起架來，打得不可開交，直到彼此都眼冒金星、半死不活地倒在地上。狐狸從旁邊經過，看見獅子和熊並排躺着，中間有一頭鹿。狐狸抓起鹿，拔腿就溜。它們兩個都沒有力氣爬起來，只能小聲嘀咕："我們真倒霉！沒想到卻讓狐狸撿了便宜！"

這則寓言說明：眼看自己努力過後得到的成果被別人拿走，心裏自然不是滋味。

70
獅子和兔子

獅子發現了一隻熟睡的兔子，正想吃掉它，忽然間看到邊上跑來一頭鹿。獅子就扔下兔子去追鹿。兔子聽到響聲，醒了過來，連忙逃跑了。獅子費了好長時間追鹿，卻始終捉不住它，於是回過頭來找兔子。當它發現兔子已經不見了時，失望地說：“我真是活該！到手的獵物被我放掉，卻去追求希望渺茫的東西。”

有些人也是如此，好高騖遠，不滿現狀，沒想到連已經擁有的也失去了。

71
獅子、驢子和狐狸

獅子、驢子和狐狸決定生活在一起，合夥去打獵。它們捕獲了許多獵物，獅子就吩咐驢子來分配成果。驢子把獵物平均分成三份，請獅子先挑。獅子大動肝火，把驢子咬死了，接着又命令狐狸來分。狐狸把大部分獵物都歸成一堆，留給自己的只有很小一部分，並讓獅子先挑。獅子問狐狸，是誰教它分得如此公平合理的？狐狸回答："是死去的驢子！"

這則寓言說明：對人類來說，別人的不幸是前車之鑒。

獅子和老鼠

獅子正在睡大覺，一隻老鼠爬到了它的身上。獅子醒了，一把抓住老鼠，要把它吃掉。老鼠哀求獅子放了它，並且答應今後一定以德報德，答謝它的饒命之恩，獅子哈哈大笑，放了老鼠。誰知沒過多久老鼠真的救了獅子的命，答謝了它。一次，獅子落入獵人的手中，他們用繩子把它綁在樹上，老鼠聽到了獅子的呻吟，立刻跑來，咬斷了繩子，把它救出來。救獅子之前老鼠對它這麼說："當初你取笑我，似乎不相信我能夠回報你的善舉；現在你知道了吧，連老鼠也有能力知恩圖報。"

這則寓言說明，有時候命運變化莫測，甚至強者也需要弱者的幫忙。

73
狼羣和羊羣

狼羣打算襲擊羊羣,可是一直沒機會,因為有好幾條狗一直在保護羊羣。於是,狼決定用計謀來達到目的。它們派出幾個使者到羊那兒去,慫恿羊羣把狗趕走,表示都是因為狗的介入,才使它們之間彼此仇視;要是把狗趕走的話,那麼狼和羊之間就能和平共處。羊羣完全沒有考慮到後果,就這樣把狗給趕走了。結果如此一來,狼就毫無顧忌了,輕而易舉就將整羣羊都吃下肚。

國家也是如此,把人民的領袖拱手出賣給敵人,就意味着將要面臨失敗。

74
狼和小綿羊

狼看到小綿羊在喝小溪裏的水，打算找個得體的藉口把小綿羊吃掉。它站在溪水的上游，開始責備小綿羊，説都是因為小綿羊把水攪渾了，才讓它不能喝。小綿羊回答，它只用嘴唇輕輕碰了一下水，而且也不可能把狼要喝的水攪渾，因為自己站的地方是小溪的下游。眼看自己的陰謀不能得逞，狼便説："不過去年你用粗話辱罵過我的父親！"小綿羊回答説，去年它還沒出世呢。於是狼説道："不管你怎麼狡猾地為自己辯解，反正我要把你吃掉！"

這則寓言説明：下了決心要做壞事的人，任何東西也阻擋不了。

75

狼和白鷺

狼給骨頭卡住了喉嚨,四處尋求協助。它遇見了白鷺,就對它許諾說,要是能幫自己把骨頭拔出來,一定給它獎賞。白鷺把腦袋伸進狼的喉嚨,拔出了骨頭,然後向狼要獎賞。可是狼卻回答說:"你的腦袋安然無恙地從狼的嘴裏出來,這還不夠嗎,還想要甚麼獎賞?"

這則寓言説明:壞人認為自己一次不做壞事就是對人天大的恩賜。

狼和山羊

狼看見一隻山羊在懸崖上吃草，它想爬到山羊身邊，可是無能為力。於是，它就懇求山羊從懸崖上下來，狼對山羊説：在懸崖上一不小心就會摔下來，底下這裏有一片草地，有一大堆嫩草。可是山羊回答：“不，問題不在於我到你那裏去可以吃到鮮嫩的青草，而在於你在那兒沒東西可吃。”

當壞人企圖做壞事、加害好人時，他們的一切陰謀詭計都無法得逞。

77
算命先生

算命先生在廣場上為人看相，預測未來，掙錢過活。忽然，有個人朝他跑過來，大聲喊着強盜砸開了他家的門，搶走了所有的財產。算命先生大驚失色，一躍而起，哀號着拼命往家裏跑，想看看發生了甚麼事。有個過路人見此情景便問："老兄，既然你對自己的事情都一無所知，那又如何預測別人的事情呢？"

這則寓言針對那些自己不會生活，卻愛多管閒事的人。

男孩和渡鴉

有個婦人去為自己年幼的兒子算命，算命先生告訴她，渡鴉會為她兒子帶來厄運。婦人驚恐萬狀，準備了一個大箱子把兒子藏在裏面，想以此來保護他免遭渡鴉的襲擊、躲避死神。只有吃飯時她才會打開箱子，為兒子送上食物。有一天，她打開箱子讓兒子進食，兒子不小心探出身子，結果門上那把鎖掉在他的頭上，把他砸死了。

這則寓言說明，命運的安排是躲避不了的。

79
鼴鼠和銀鼠

鼴鼠與銀鼠交戰，鼴鼠吃了敗仗。有一天，鼴鼠們聚在一起商量對策，一致斷定它們的失敗是因為羣龍無首。於是它們選出了幾個統帥，並把它們高舉在頭上。統帥們為了顯得與眾不同，搞來一些牛角綁在自己頭上。激戰開始了，鼴鼠再次失利。普通的鼴鼠一下子鑽進鼠洞，四處逃命，輕而易舉地躲藏了起來；而那些統帥們由於頭上綁着牛角，無法鑽進洞裏，被銀鼠抓住，徹底完蛋了。

虛榮心會給許多人帶來不幸。

遇難的人和大海

有個人乘船遠航，途中大船傾覆，他好不容易遊到了海岸邊，已經筋疲力盡，他倒頭就睡。不一會，他醒過來，看見大海，對着它破口大罵，罵它起先風平浪靜，笑臉相迎，引誘人們出海，一旦人們啟航，它就立刻兇相畢露，興風作浪，讓人們葬身海底。這時，大海變成了女人的模樣，對人說："親愛的，你不該罵我，應該去向大風問罪！我生來就是你見到的這副模樣，可是，風突然颳到我身上，我才變得如此瘋狂和兇暴。"

最可惡的不是登上前台的跳梁小丑，而是那些躲在幕後的策劃者。

81
蝙蝠、荊棘和海鷗

蝙蝠、荊棘和海鷗決定合夥做買賣。蝙蝠負責借錢，作為公司的成本，荊棘貢獻自己的衣服，海鷗帶來一大堆銅，準備作為商品出售。可是當它們乘船航行時，突然狂風大作，船被掀翻了。它們三個好不容易爬到了陸地上，可船上所有的貨物和商品都不見蹤影。之後海鷗為了尋找那些銅，一次次潛入深海中。蝙蝠生怕給債主看到，於是白天都躲藏起來，等到夜裏才飛出去覓食；而荊棘則是整天在尋找自己失去的衣服，看到有人路過就抓住人家的衣服不放，想看看別人身上有沒有自己的衣服。

這則寓言說明，我們最關心的莫過於自己遭受的損失。

蝙蝠和銀鼠

蝙蝠倒在地上，銀鼠上前抓住它，發現它已經氣息奄奄。蝙蝠哀求銀鼠饒了它，銀鼠回答沒辦法，因為自己生來就同一切鳥類為敵。可是蝙蝠說，它不是鳥類而是鼠類，於是銀鼠就把它放了。另一次，蝙蝠又倒在地上，另外一隻銀鼠抓住了它。蝙蝠哀求銀鼠不要殺害自己，因為它不是鼠類，而是飛行動物，銀鼠又放了它。就這樣，蝙蝠兩次改名換姓，才得以保全性命。

不能墨守成規，善於隨機應變常常能避免天災人禍。

83
樵夫和赫耳墨斯

一個樵夫在河岸上砍柴，不慎把斧頭掉入河中。河水沖走了斧頭，樵夫坐在岸邊失聲痛哭。赫耳墨斯可憐他，來到他跟前，了解了樵夫傷心的原因。赫耳墨斯潛入水中，為樵夫取出了一把金斧頭，問他是不是這把？樵夫回答說，不是這把。赫耳墨斯再次進到水裏，取出一把銀斧頭，又問他，這是不是他丟失的斧頭？樵夫又否認了。於是，赫耳墨斯第三次下水，為他取回了真正屬於他的木頭斧頭，樵夫認了這把斧頭。赫耳墨斯為了獎勵樵夫的誠實，將三把斧頭全都送給了他。樵夫拿了禮物，便去找朋友們，向大家講述了事情的全部過程。有一個朋友非常嫉妒，便想依樣畫葫蘆。他拿了一把斧頭來到那條小河邊，揮起斧頭砍起樹來，他故意將斧頭掉入河中，然後坐下來，開始哭泣。赫耳墨斯來了，問他發生了甚麼事？他回答說，斧頭掉了。赫耳墨斯為他取出一把金斧頭，問他，這是不是他丟失的那把斧頭？貪婪使這個人失去了理智，他大聲喊道，正是那把斧頭。但是，神不但不給他獎勵，而且連他自己的那把斧頭也沒還給他。

這則寓言說明，眾神總是幫助誠實的人，鄙視不誠實的人。

農夫和蛇

隆冬季節，一位農夫在路上行走，看見一條凍僵的蛇。他可憐這條蛇，就把它抱起來，放到自己懷裏暖着。當蛇凍僵時，它安安分分地躺着，等到它緩過來以後，便朝農夫肚子上咬了一口。農夫預感到死亡將臨，說道："我這是活該，何必去救奄奄一息的壞蛋呢，這種壞東西即便活着，也得把它消滅掉！"

這則寓言說明：惡人不僅不會以德報德，而且還會恩將仇報、加害自己的救命恩人。

85
兩個旅人

兩個旅人在海岸邊行走，他們爬上一個小山坡，看見遠處海上漂浮着一捆樹枝，兩人以為是一艘大船，便耐心等待大船靠岸。等到大風把樹枝吹近些，他們斷定這是一個木筏，只是比看起來的要小，兩人繼續等待。最後，樹枝靠了岸，他們這才終於看清楚是甚麼東西，於是其中一人說道："我們白白等了這麼久，結果卻令人大失所望！"

有些人遠看似乎威嚴可怕，等到走近一看，原來不堪一擊。

馱鹽的驢子

驢子馱着鹽過河,不小心腳一滑,跌倒在河裏。鹽溶化了,驢子感到輕鬆了,它暗自高興。又一次,它馱着海綿走向小河,心裏盤算着:要是它再次滑倒,那就又能減輕負擔,輕裝上路。於是它故意滑倒。結果,海綿浸了水,膨脹開來,驢子爬不起來,在河裏淹死了。

有些人也是如此,機關用盡,不料聰明反被聰明誤,最後自食其果。

87
馱着雕像的驢子

有個人把一尊神的雕像放在驢子背上讓它馱着進城。誰見了這尊雕像都朝它深深地鞠躬。驢子斷定大家這是在向它自己鞠躬，就神氣活現起來，並大聲嚷嚷，不願繼續往前走。趕驢的人猜到了是怎麼回事，一邊用棍子打它，一邊説：“你這個傻瓜！讓人向驢子鞠躬，簡直是豈有此理！”

這則寓言説明，靠別人的功勞炫耀自己的人們，隨着時間的推移，會遭到所有熟人的恥笑。

驢子和蟬

驢子聽到蟬持續不斷的鳴叫聲，非常喜歡這種美妙的歌聲，就羨慕起蟬來，問道：“你都吃甚麼食物才會擁有這麼好的嗓子？”“露水，”蟬答道。於是，驢子也開始只喝露水，可是最後卻因此而餓死了。

人類也是如此，做違背自己天性的事情，不僅不能達到目的，而且還會大禍臨頭。

89
驢子和狼

驢子在草地上吃草，忽然看見一條狼朝自己跑來。驢子假裝跛腳，一瘸一瘸地走着。狼跑到它跟前，問它為甚麼瘸着走路。驢子回答："攀籬笆時腳上扎了刺！"它請求狼先幫自己把腳上的刺拔掉，然後再吃它，免得被扎傷。狼相信了驢子的話，驢子抬起腳，狼開始仔細察看驢的蹄子，可是驢子猛地用蹄子對準狼的臉踢去，狼所有的牙齒全都給踢掉了。狼疼痛不堪，小聲說道："我這是活該！父親培養我食肉為生，我根本不是做醫生的料！"

人類也是如此，有些人總是逞強好勝，幹不適合自己的事情。

驢子、狐狸和獅子

驢子和狐狸決定和睦相處,一起出發去打獵,半路上遇到一頭獅子。狐狸見情況危急,連忙跑到獅子跟前,答應只要獅子不碰它,就一定幫忙把驢子交給獅子。獅子答應放了狐狸;於是,狐狸將驢子誘騙到獅子跟前。獅子見驢子已經逃脫不了,就先把狐狸撕成碎塊,然後再撲向驢子。

想害人,結果往往先害己。

91

捕鳥人和鸛

捕鳥人設下了陷阱，躲在遠處觀察着捕鳥的經過。鸛和鶴一起來到田裏，捕鳥人見了連忙跑過來，把兩隻鳥一起抓了起來。鸛拼命哀求捕鳥人不要殺它，因為它對人類不僅沒有害處，而且還有益處，會捕捉和消滅蛇與其他有害的動物。捕鳥人反駁説："即使你能給人類帶來三倍的利益也無濟於事，因為你在這兒跟壞蛋同流合污，所以，你還是得受懲罰。"

交友應當謹慎，免得被其他人視為同謀。

駱駝

人們第一次見到駱駝時，被它高大的身材嚇得驚恐萬分，四處奔逃。可是過了一段時間，他們了解到駱駝性格溫順，慢慢地膽子便大了起來，開始接近它。又過了一些日子，人們明白了駱駝根本就不會發脾氣，就開始非常鄙視駱駝，甚至給它套上韁繩，讓孩子們牽着玩耍。

這則寓言說明，習慣足以克服原先的恐懼。

偷東西的男孩和他的母親

有個男孩上課時偷了同學的寫字板，帶回家交給母親，他的母親非但沒有懲罰他，還誇獎他一番。於是第二次他又偷了別人的斗篷交給母親，母親更加高興。光陰荏苒，男孩子長成了一個青年，偷竊的行為也跟着變本加厲。最後，有一次當他行竊時，被當場抓住，給人家捆住胳膊，押赴刑場。他的母親跟在後面，傷心地捶胸頓足。這時候他對母親說想跟她說句悄悄話。母親走到他身邊，誰知他一口咬掉了母親的耳朵。母親罵他是個逆子，他犯下的罪還嫌不夠多嗎，連自己的親生母親也不放過！兒子打斷她的話說："要是你在我第一次把偷來的寫字板交給你時就懲罰我，那我也就不會變成今天這個樣子，也不會被押赴刑場。"

這則寓言說明：小錯不改，大誤即來。

猴子和漁夫們

大樹上有隻猴子，看到漁夫們往河裏撒網，便悄悄地觀察着他們的一舉一動。當漁夫們把網拉上來，遠遠的坐着吃早飯時，猴子便從樹上跳下來，想學漁夫撒網的樣子，自己動手捉魚，也難怪人們常說猴子是善於模仿的動物。可是，它才剛拿起魚網，就被困在裏面；它於是自言自語地說："我這是活該！既然不知道怎樣捕魚，何必硬要逞強呢？"

這則寓言說明，逞強好勝，班門弄斧，有害無益。

95
牧羊人和羊羣

牧羊人將自己的羊羣趕到小樹林裏,看到那兒有一棵高大的橡樹,上面結滿了橡實。他解開身上的斗篷鋪在地上,然後爬到樹上大力搖晃。不料,底下的羊羣卻把這些橡實吃了個精光,而且最後還把斗篷也一起吃下肚。牧羊人從樹上爬下來,看到發生的事,便說道:"你們這些惡毒的東西!為甚麼你們獻出羊毛給其他人做斗篷,而我這個飼養你們的人,卻連自己的舊斗篷也要被你們奪去?"

世上很多人都愚不可及,對外人卑躬屈膝,對自己人卻肆無忌憚。

撒謊取樂的牧羊人

牧羊人趕着自己的羊羣離開了村莊，到遠處去休息。他老是喜歡撒謊取樂。他常常高聲大叫，謊稱狼在追趕羊，招呼農民前來幫忙。前兩次，農民信以為真，嚇得連忙趕來救助，可是當他們到的時候，卻發現只是一場玩笑。後來有一次，狼真的來了。狼開始咬羊，牧羊人又喊着向農民求助。但這次大家都認為這又是牧羊人在愚弄大家，所以無人反應。結果，牧羊人就失去了他所有的羊。

這則寓言說明，撒謊的人總會得到報應，即使說的是真話也沒人會相信。

鼴鼠

　　　隻瞎眼的鼴鼠有一天對媽媽説：“我復明了！”鼴鼠媽媽決
　　　定檢驗一下兒子説得對不對，給了它一粒神香並問道：“這
是甚麼？”鼴鼠回答：“這是一粒小石子。”媽媽對它説：“我的孩
子，你不僅沒有復明，現在連嗅覺也不靈了！”

愛説大話的人總是承諾自己辦不到的事情，實際上他們連小事做
不好。

胡蜂和蛇

胡蜂停留在蛇的頭上不停地蜇它，弄得它不得安寧。蛇痛得難以忍受，可是又沒有辦法做甚麼來報復。蛇只好爬出洞，來到大路上，看見一輛大車駛過來，將頭一伸，朝輪子底下鑽去。蛇和胡蜂同歸於盡，臨死前蛇說道："雖然我即將命赴黃泉，但能與仇敵同歸於盡，我在所不惜。"

這則寓言針對那些甘願與敵人同歸於盡的人。

99
猴子的孩子

傳說猴子生了一對雙胞胎，其中一個孩子受到父母的寵愛，得到精心照料，而另一個孩子卻遭到父母的厭惡，得不到任何關心。然而，命運的安排卻頗為神妙：得寵的孩子夭折了，而那個失寵的卻活了下來。

這則寓言說明，命運的安排勝過任何關愛。

100
孔雀和寒鴉

鳥兒們開會商量，選誰做大王。孔雀堅決要求大家選它為王，因為它長得漂亮。大家正打算同意，不料，寒鴉開了腔："要是你當了大王，那麼老雕來襲擊我們的時候，你如何救大家？"

這則寓言說的是，為統治者增光的不是美貌，而是力量。

101
駱駝、大象和猴子

動物們開會商量，選誰做大王，大象和駱駝搶着發言，爭論不休，它們都自以為比所有的動物高大，有力氣。但是猴子卻認為它們兩個都不適合當大王，因為駱駝不會對惡霸發怒，而大象看到小豬來侵犯也束手無策，因為大象怕小豬。

這則寓言說明，小障礙往往會妨礙大事業。

102
野豬和狐狸

野豬站在樹底下磨獠牙，狐狸問它這是幹甚麼？既沒有獵人來，也不見有甚麼其他災禍，何必磨牙呢？野豬回答說："我磨牙並不會徒勞，大禍臨頭時，我就不必再'臨陣磨槍'了，因為我早已經準備好了。"

這則寓言告誡人們，有備無患。

103
守財奴

有個守財奴把所有家當都變賣成現金，買了金塊，藏在牆角底下；之後每天都會來這兒看看，過過癮。附近有許多人在幹活，其中一人發現了守財奴奇怪的舉動，猜到了是怎麼回事。於是，趁守財奴不在的時候，他就偷走了金塊。金塊的主人回來後，看到埋金塊的地方空空如也，傷心地號啕大哭起來。有人見他這副悲痛欲絕的樣子，立刻明白了事情的緣由，對他説："別傷心了，拿一塊石頭放在那個地方，幻想這是金塊，不就成了？因為金塊放在這裏的時候，你並沒有好好利用。"

這則寓言説明，不用的財富一文不值。

烏龜和兔子

烏龜同兔子爭論，誰跑得快。它們定下比賽的時間和地點，雙方同時起跑。兔子仗着自己天生跑得快，沒有使勁奔跑，卻躺在路邊睡起大覺來。而烏龜意識到自己行動緩慢，不停地拼命奔跑。於是，烏龜就超過了睡大覺的兔子。

這則寓言説明，縱使擁有天賦，若是不能善加利用或太過驕傲自滿，常常會敗給努力。

105
燕子和蛇

燕子在法院屋頂下築了個巢。有一天當它飛出去時，蛇爬進了燕巢，把它的小寶寶吃得一隻不剩。燕子回來，看到家裏空蕩蕩的，傷心地哭了起來。其他燕子都紛紛想辦法安慰它，要它知道自己並不是唯一失去孩子的家長。可是燕子回答説：“我並不是為孩子們哭泣，我傷心的是我在其他受害者能夠得到援助的地方成了受害者。”

這則寓言説明，意料之外的傷害往往最令人難以承受。

106
白鵝和仙鶴

白鵝和仙鶴在一塊草地上吃草，突然來了幾個獵人；輕巧的仙鶴翅膀一拍，飛上了天空，而白鵝身體笨重，動作緩慢，成了俘虜。

人也是如此：當一個國家發生動亂時，窮人輕裝上路，說走就走，得以逃命，富人家財萬貫，欲走不成，最後卻淪為奴隸。

107
燕子和烏鴉

燕子同烏鴉爭論,誰長得美麗。烏鴉對燕子説:"你的美麗只在春天才能顯示出來,而我的身體即使到了冬天也照樣能經受考驗。"

這則寓言説明,人萬萬不能只注重外表。

烏龜和老雕

烏龜看到空中有一隻老雕，十分羨慕，也想試着飛上天。它朝着老雕爬去，求它教教自己，無論花多大代價都行。老雕説這辦不到。可是烏龜一再懇求，老雕只好答應了。於是，老雕叼着烏龜上了天，把它帶到高空，再扔到懸崖上。烏龜撲通一聲摔得粉身碎骨，一命嗚呼了。

這則寓言説的是，許多人渴望與人較量，卻忘了聽取勸告，最後自取滅亡。

109
門德雷斯河畔的狐狸

門德雷斯河是一條位於土耳其西南部的河流，源頭是安納托利亞高原，注入愛琴海。河畔住着一羣狐狸。有一天，狐狸們聚集在門德雷斯河畔，打算暢飲一番；可是河水嘩嘩地流淌，聲音震耳欲聾，雖然大家互相鼓勁，卻沒有一隻狐狸敢下河。這時，其中一隻狐狸想挑戰其他狐狸，於是走到最前方，開始嘲笑同伴們膽小，而它自己以勇敢而自豪，毫無畏懼地跳入水中。水流把它沖到河中央，其他狐狸站在岸邊，對它大聲喊道：“別離開我們，回來吧，告訴我們怎樣跳到水裏才安全？”那只被水沖走的狐狸回答說：“我有個訊息要送到米萊圖斯，那是一個位於小亞細亞愛奧尼亞的古城，也是古代商業、手工業和文化中心。我得親自去一趟。等我回來後再教你們吧！”

這則寓言針對愛說大話而自食其果的人。

天鵝

傳說天鵝臨死前都要唱歌。有個人在市場上看見有人在販售天鵝，就掏錢買了一隻，這樣他就能盡情地享受美妙歌聲。一天，這個人請客吃飯，在宴席上他叫天鵝唱歌，可是天鵝不答應。然而，後來沒過多久，天鵝預感到自己死期將臨，便扯開嗓子，唱起了悲歌。聽到歌聲，主人說道："我真是傻瓜，早知你只肯在臨死前唱歌，那麼我當時不該叫你唱歌，而該把你宰了。"

有些人也是如此，不見棺材不落淚。

111
狼和牧羊人

狼跟在羊羣後面,但是沒有傷害它們。一開始牧羊人把狼當成敵人,對它十分警惕,小心地守候着。可是見狼始終跟在羊羣後面,卻沒有向羊進攻,牧羊人就斷定,自己遇到的狼不會傷害羊羣,甚至還會保護它們。當他有事要到城裏去時,就把羊羣託付給狼去看管,然後放心地走了。狼知道,機會來了,它痛痛快快地咬死了幾乎所有的羊。牧羊人回來,發現他的羊全都死了,便說:"我這是活該:怎麼能把羊託付給狼呢?"

人也是如此,往往把自己的財產交給貪婪的小人,之後喪失財產只能怨自己。

螞蟻和鴿子

螞蟻口渴，來到泉水邊想暢飲一番，不料掉進了水裏。鴿子從附近的樹上扯下一片葉子扔給螞蟻。螞蟻好容易爬到葉子上，得救了。這時，不遠處有個獵人停下腳步，準備好箭，正打算逮住鴿子。螞蟻出其不意地在獵人腿上猛咬一口，他一驚，手裏拿着的箭一抖，鴿子聽到動靜，趁機飛走了。

這則寓言說明，有時候弱者也能幫助別人。

113
兩個旅人和渡鴉

兩個人趕着去辦事，半路上遇到一隻獨眼渡鴉，他們就一直跟在它後面，其中一個人提議乾脆回去算了，他覺得這只渡鴉是個不祥之兆。但另一個人卻反駁道："渡鴉怎麼能預測未來呢？它連自己受傷致殘都無法預料和防備。"

人類也是如此，平庸無能的人，無法給予他人意見。

買驢

有個人準備購買一頭驢，他想先測試一下，便把這頭驢帶回家，讓它跟自己家裏養着的另外幾頭驢一起挨着飼料槽。這頭驢一來就不學好，整天和家裏最好吃懶做的驢在一起，對其他驢連正眼都不瞧一下。這個人看了後二話不說，抓起驢身上繫着的繩子就出門把驢還給了賣主。賣主問，測試的結果怎麼樣？買驢人回答說：“我不用做任何測試了，因為我看見這頭驢選擇了甚麼樣的夥伴，我就明白了。”

這則寓言說明，物以類聚，人以羣分，看人要看他交甚麼朋友。

115
家鴿和野鴿

捕鳥人撒開網，將幾隻家鴿綁在網上，自己卻離得遠遠的，在遠處等候。野鴿飛到家鴿身邊，卻跟着一起被困在網中，捕鳥人跑過去逮住它們。野鴿責怪家鴿沒有提醒同伴有陷阱，可是家鴿反駁道："不，對我們來說最重要的是不違背主人，而不是關心自己的同類。"

忠義難兩全。

管錢的人和誓言

有個人受朋友之託，代為保管一筆錢，可他見錢眼開，想把這筆錢佔為己有。朋友曾經要他發誓；他不敢發誓，提心吊膽地啟程回家。在城門口他看見一個瘸子從城裏出來，就問他是甚麼人，要到哪裏去。瘸子回答說，是誓言召喚他去追捕違背誓言的人。負責保管錢的人又問瘸子，何時還會再到城裏來，瘸子說："也許四十年，也可能三十年。"於是這個人就不再為將來擔憂，立刻折回去向朋友發了誓：託自己保管的錢，自己絕對不會起貪念，據為己有。他話音剛落，誓言就盯上了他，緊緊跟在他後面，想把他從懸崖上扔下去。他抱怨起來，怪誓言說話不算數，本來答應過三十年後再回來，可是連一天時間也沒有給他。誓言回答說："記住，要是有人背叛我，犯了錯，那麼我馬上就會回來。"

這則寓言說明，懲罰壞人，不會事先通知。

117
普羅米修斯和人類

普羅米修斯按宙斯的吩咐用泥塑成了人類和動物，但是宙斯發現，其中無知的動物太多，就命令普羅米修斯把一部分動物毀掉，重新塑造成人。普羅米修斯服從了命令，結果那些由動物塑造成的人雖然有人的外貌，但他們體內卻留着野獸的心。

這則寓言針對粗魯、愚蠢的人。

蟬和狐狸

蟬在大樹上唱歌，狐狸想吃掉它，就耍了個花招。狐狸站在大樹跟前，開始對蟬阿諛奉承，說它嗓音美妙，歌聲悅耳，並懇求它到樹下來，自己想看看究竟是誰歌唱得這麼動聽。蟬猜到了狐狸的詭計，便從樹上扯下一片樹葉丟了下去。狐狸連忙撲上去，以為是蟬。蟬便說道："狐狸大哥，要是你癡心妄想我會下樹，那你就錯了。自從之前我在其他狐狸的糞便裏發現了蟬的翅膀後，我就開始對狐狸小心提防了。"

這則寓言說明有智慧的人會從他人的不幸中吸取教訓。

鸚鵡和銀鼠

有個人買了一隻鸚鵡，讓它住在自己家裏。鸚鵡漸漸習慣了他家的生活，常常飛到爐灶上，隨便一躺，就用自己洪亮的嗓子嘰嘰喳喳叫起來。銀鼠看到鸚鵡，問它是誰，從哪裏來。鸚鵡回答說："我是主人不久前剛買回來的。"銀鼠說："厚顏無恥的東西！你才被買來，就這麼神氣活現地亂叫！而我，儘管從出生起就生活在這個家裏，但連吱吱叫幾聲主人都不允許，只要我一發出聲音，他們就火冒三丈，把我趕跑。"鸚鵡聽了說道："你滾一邊去吧，你要知道，我的嗓音才不像你的嗓音那麼讓主人討厭。"

這則寓言針對愛吵嘴的人，這種人總是盛氣凌人地一味指責別人。

120
母獅和狐狸

狐狸責備母獅，説它只生了一個孩子，母獅反駁道：“儘管是一個，但卻是有頭有臉的雄獅。”

這則寓言説明，重要的不是數量，而是質量。

121
狼和小綿羊

狼追捕小綿羊，小綿羊跑進了神廟，狼叫它出來，說要是祭司抓住了它，就會把它當作祭品獻給神祇。小綿羊回答說："我寧可做神的祭品，也不願被你殺死。"

這則寓言說明，如果難逃一死，最好死得體面。

驢子和騾子

驢子和騾子一起在路上走，驢子見它們兩個馱的貨一樣多，就氣憤地抱怨起來，說騾子馱的貨比自己少，可吃的東西卻比自己多一倍。它們沒走多少路，趕牲口的人就發現驢子已經不堪重負，於是，他從驢子身上拿下一部分貨物放到騾子身上。又走了一段路，他發現驢子更加筋疲力盡，便又從驢子身上拿掉一部分貨物。就這樣，走一段，減一些，直到把驢子身上的所有貨物都加在騾子身上。這時候，騾子回過頭來對驢子說："老弟，我用自己的勞動堂堂正正地掙來了雙倍口糧，你呢？"

看事情不能只看開頭，不看結果。

123
兩個袋子

普羅米修斯塑造了人類之後，在每個人的肩上掛了兩個袋子：一個裝着別人的毛病，另一個裝着自己的。普羅米修斯把裝着自己毛病的袋子掛在人的背後，而裝着別人毛病的袋子則掛在人的胸前。結果造成人類總是先看見別人的問題，卻忘了自己的缺點。

這則寓言可以用來諷刺好奇心重的人，這種人對自己的事情一竅不通，對別人的事情卻十分熱中。

124
蠕蟲和蛇

蠕蟲看見路上躺着一條蛇，十分羨慕："它長得可真大呀。" 蠕蟲希望自己也能像蛇一樣，於是也躺在一旁，挺直身子，不斷拉長，直到身體用力過大突然斷成兩截為止。

有些人也常常如此，老是想同強者較量，結果出師未捷身先死。

125
野豬、馬和獵人

野豬和馬同在一塊草地上吃草。野豬每次都把馬要吃的草踩爛，把它要喝的水攪渾。馬為了報復野豬，跑去找獵人幫忙。獵人說，只要馬願意戴上韁繩，讓自己騎到它背上，他就願意幫忙。馬答應了所有條件。獵人跳上馬，戰勝了野豬，接着把馬騎回自己家裏，繫在牲口槽上。

許多人也是如此，一心只想着報復敵人，結果到頭來自己也成了他人的階下囚。

蚊子和獅子

蚊子飛到獅子跟前挑釁説："我不怕你,你沒有我厲害!想想吧,你的勇猛表現在哪裏?是有爪子可以抓人家,還是有牙齒能咬人家呢?這種事任何一個太太跟先生打架時都做得到。我可比你厲害多了!要是你願意,我們來比試比試!"蚊子大叫一聲,沖向獅子,在它臉上叮了一口。獅子抬起自己的爪子開始抓臉,直到筋疲力盡,怒不可遏。蚊子戰勝了獅子,高唱着勝利的凱歌飛走了。可是這時它忽然落入蜘蛛網中,無可奈何地歎息着咽了氣。蚊子戰勝了最強大的敵人,卻因微不足道的蜘蛛而喪了命。

這則寓言針對能夠戰勝大人物,卻敗在小人物手下的人。

127
樵夫和橡樹

樵夫在砍一棵橡樹，他們先用橡樹做成楔子，再用楔子撐開樹幹。橡樹說："我能夠忍受斧頭砍在身上的痛楚，但是用我身體的一部分來謀害我，這一點實在令人難以接受。"

這則寓言說明，受到親人的欺負比受到外人的欺負更令人痛苦。

松樹和荊棘

松樹高傲地對荊棘說:"你毫無用處,而我可以用來蓋房子,做神廟的屋頂。"荊棘反駁說:"你這個可憐蟲,還是回想一下斧頭和鋸子是如何折磨你的吧,你當初還想變成荊棘呢。"

沒有危險的貧窮勝過充滿悲傷和不安的富有。

129
人和獅子同行

獅子和人一起在路上走。人揚言：“人比獅子厲害！”獅子反駁：“獅子比人厲害！”他們繼續往前走，人指着一塊刻着一隻被人制服、踩在腳下的獅子的石板，說道：“看到沒有，這就是獅子最後的下場！”可是獅子又反駁說：“要是獅子會雕刻的話，那麼石頭上面刻着的可就是完全不一樣的情況了。”

這則寓言說的是，有些人只會出一張嘴，卻毫無能力可言。

狗和蝸牛

有一條狗很愛吃蛋。一次，它看到一隻蝸牛，以為是蛋，便張大嘴巴，猛地一口吞下了肚。可是它頓時感到胃不太舒服，説道："我真是活該受罪，怎麼能以為凡是圓的東西都是蛋呢？"

這則寓言告誡我們，做事不三思而行的人往往會誤入險境。

131
狗、狐狸和公雞

狗和公雞決定和睦相處，一同結伴啟程上路。夜裏，它們來到一個小樹林，公雞飛到樹上，在樹枝間安頓下來，狗在下面的樹洞裏沉沉入睡。黑夜過去了，天邊出現了曙光，公雞照老習慣大聲啼叫起來。狐狸聽到了公雞的叫聲，想把公雞當成早餐。它走過來，站在樹下對公雞喊道："你是討人喜歡的家禽，對人類有益！請下來吧，讓我們一起來哼一首小夜曲，我們兩個一定會心情舒暢，快樂無比！"可是公雞對它説："過來吧，親愛的，走得近一點，把那樹邊底下的守衛叫來，讓他擊樹為我們伴奏。"狐狸走過來，剛想去叫守衛，不料狗兒猛地撲到狐狸身上，一把抓住它，把它撕得粉碎。

這則寓言説明，當聰明人遇到危險時，善於利用智慧化險為夷。

雲雀

雲雀有一天落入了陷阱，它一邊痛哭，一邊說："我真是一個可憐又倒霉的小鳥！我既沒有偷過金，也沒有偷過銀，甚麼值錢的東西也沒有偷過，卻為了一顆小穀粒而送了命。"

這則寓言針對貪小失大的人。

133
狼和狗

狼看見一條大狗脖子上戴着用鐵製成的項圈，便問："是誰把你鎖起來又把你養得這麼肥的？"狗回答說："獵人。"狼說："感謝老天沒讓這種事發生在我們狼的身上！我們既不需要擔心飢餓也不必煩惱沉重項圈的束縛。"

身陷不幸，食不甘味。

驢子和狗

驢子和狗一起在路上走，它們發現地上有一封封了口的信。驢子撿起信，拆了封，打開信念給狗聽。信中說的是關於牲口飼料的事情：乾草、大麥、麥秸。狗對驢子讀的內容很反感，它對驢子說："朋友，跳過些內容行嗎？或許後面能找到幾句關於肉和骨頭的句子？"驢子瀏覽了整封信，可是狗想聽的話一句也沒找到。於是狗說："朋友，把這封信重新扔回地上吧，裏面甚麼有用的東西也沒有。"

不同的人興趣不同，不能強求。

135
獅子、狼和狐狸

獅子年邁力衰，躺在山洞裏一病不起。所有野獸都紛紛前來探望它們的大王，惟獨狐狸沒有露面。狼利用這個機會，在獅子面前搬弄是非，誹謗狐狸："它呀，根本就沒把獸王放在眼裏，所以才不來探望。"狐狸恰好這時候趕到，狼最後説的兩句話它全聽到了。獅子對着狐狸大聲咆哮；狐狸連忙請求給它機會解釋。"聚集在這裏的所有大小野獸，"狐狸感慨地説道，"誰像我這麼盡心盡力地幫你？為了你的病，我到處奔波，找遍了所有的醫生，終於為你打聽到了治病的好方法。"獅子立刻吩咐它説説到底是甚麼方法。狐狸回答説："你得把狼皮活剝下來，裹在身上！"當狼挺直身子，奄奄一息地躺在地上時，狐狸挖苦它説："不該慫恿大王作惡，應該勸它行善。"

這則寓言説明：誰陰謀害人，終究會自食惡果。

埃塞俄比亞人

有個人買下一個埃塞俄比亞人，他以為，埃塞俄比亞人皮膚這麼黑是由於原先主人的過失，因此，當他把埃塞俄比亞人一帶回到家裏，立刻就用大量的水和強鹼溶液為他沖洗。可是那人的皮膚絲毫也沒有改變，反而由於他的折騰，埃塞俄比亞人病倒了。

這則寓言說明，一個人天生的模樣是改變不了的。

妻子和酒鬼丈夫

有個女人的丈夫是個酒鬼，為了讓他戒除這個嗜好，妻子想出了一條妙計。等到丈夫酒足飯飽，進入夢鄉，像死人一樣不省人事的時候，她就把丈夫扛到墓地，丟下就走。她估計丈夫該睡醒的時候，又跑到墓地去敲門。丈夫問："誰在敲門？""是我，"妻子答道，"給死人送吃的來了！"丈夫說："我不吃，最好給我拿點喝的來，尊貴的大人！你只提到吃東西而不是喝東西，我心裏就難受。"妻子雙手捶着胸說道："我真倒霉！我的妙計全泡湯了！看來，你不但沒有醒悟，而且變得比從前更壞，已經習慣成自然了。"

這則寓言説明，對壞習慣不能聽之任之，否則總有一天壞習慣會主宰人的命運。

山羊和驢子

有個人養了一隻山羊和一頭驢子。山羊十分羨慕驢子總是給餵得飽飽的。於是山羊對驢子說："主人對你多不好啊！一會叫你推磨，一會叫你馱東西！"它慫恿驢子假裝突然生病，摔在坑裏，這樣就能歇一下。驢子聽信了山羊的話，摔在坑裏，受了傷。主人叫來獸醫，請他幫忙給驢子治傷。獸醫說："要給驢子治傷必須用山羊肺做成的膏藥，只有貼了這種膏藥驢子才能康復。"於是為了治好驢子的傷，主人就把山羊給宰了。

設計陷害別人的人往往會給自己帶來不幸。

139
牧羊人和山羊

牧羊人趕着自己飼養的山羊進羊欄。一隻山羊津津有味地啃着鮮嫩的青草，脫了隊。牧羊人撿起一塊石頭朝那只山羊扔去，不偏不倚正好擊中一個羊角，羊角給折斷了。牧羊人手足無措，戰戰兢兢地求山羊不要把這件事告訴他的東家。山羊卻說："即使我嘴裏一聲不吭也沒用，因為我頭上折斷的角是瞞不了任何人的。"

當罪行昭然若揭時，想掩蓋也沒辦法。

人和狐狸

有個人對狐狸懷着刻骨仇恨，因為狐狸毀壞了他的莊稼。這人把狐狸抓住後，打算用酷刑來懲罰它：把澆上油的麻絮綁在狐狸尾巴上，再點燃麻絮。然而神一怒之下把狐狸直接趕到了這個人的田裏；他不得不痛哭起來，因為之後這塊田裏連一粒穀子也收不到了。

人應該性格溫和，不能無節制地生氣。克制不了脾氣的人，往往會因此而承受許多不幸。

太陽的婚禮

夏日的某一天，太陽要辦喜事。所有的動物都歡天喜地，青蛙也興高采烈。可是有一隻青蛙卻說："蠢貨，有甚麼可高興的？一個太陽就把我們的沼澤地烤得這麼乾，要是太陽結了婚並且生了一個和它一樣的兒子，那我們該怎麼辦呀？"

冒失的人們常常為根本不值得高興的事情高興。

農夫和老雕

農夫在套索裏發現一隻老雕,可是老雕的美麗使他震驚,於是就把老雕放走了。後來老雕知恩圖報,它看到農夫在一堵眼看就要倒下的牆腳邊蹲下,就飛到他跟前,用爪子摘下他頭上包着的頭巾。農夫跳起來,去追老雕,老雕把頭巾扔給了他。農夫撿起來,扭頭一看,只見他待過的那堵牆轟隆一聲倒塌了,老雕的報答使農夫深受感動。

一個人受惠於別人,就該以德報德;為非作歹的人必定會自食其果。

143
小牛和老牛

小牛從未被套過牛軛，它看到耕地的老牛承受着沉重的負擔，同情地説道："唉，你吃了這麼大的苦，簡直筋疲力盡了吧？"可是老牛一聲不吭，繼續犁它的地。當農夫要給眾神上供時，就把老牛卸下套來，放它去吃草，而繩子牽着的小牛給拖過來做了犧牲品。老牛對小牛説："瞧，把你供養着是有原因的！看來你脖子上要架的不是牛軛，而是屠刀！"

勤勞踏實的人應該受到讚揚，遊手好閒的人應該受折磨、挨鞭子。

狗和廚子

有一戶人家設宴請客，家犬趁機叫來了另一條狗——它的女友，想讓它也飽飽口福。那條狗興沖沖前來赴宴，不料廚子拎起它的爪子，把它扔到外面。其他狗紛紛向它詢問宴席怎麼樣。這條狗回答說：“宴席太豐盛了，我離開那兒時，連大門都找不到了！”

由於不體面之事被趕出來的人們，常常為了面子而誇口說大話。

145
仙鶴和孔雀

金羽毛的孔雀同一身素裝的仙鶴爭論，譏笑它的羽毛太寒酸。仙鶴回答說：“可是我的翅膀能帶着我飛到星星那兒，而你像公雞一樣，只能在地上蹦蹦跳跳，任何時候天上都看不到你的影子。”

做個衣着寒酸、可敬可愛的正派人勝於成為一個穿戴華貴的卑鄙小人。

掛着小鈴鐺的狗

有一條狗老是出其不意地咬傷過路人，主人只好給它脖子上掛了一個小鈴鐺，好讓人家聽到鈴聲就躲開它。掛了小鈴鐺的狗神氣活現地來到了鬧市廣場；這時一條老狗跑過來對它說：＂你神氣甚麼呀？掛上小鈴鐺可不是件光彩的事情，而是暴露了你生性兇殘。＂

徒務虛名的陋習使愛說大話之人敗壞的道德昭然若揭。

147
膽小的獵人

有個獵人在搜尋獅子的行蹤，他問樵夫有沒有見到獅子的蹤跡或是獅子藏身的山洞？樵夫回答說："我這就指給你看一頭獅子！"獵人聽了頓時嚇得面如土色，直打寒顫，說道："不，我要找的只是獅子的蹤跡，不是真的要找獅子！"

這則寓言揭露可恥的膽小鬼，這種人口頭上勇敢，實際上卻不然。

148
狼和獅子

有一天狼從羊羣中叼走了一隻羊，把它往狼窩裏拖，可是迎面碰上了獅子，羊被獅子奪去了。狼跑了幾步，喊道："你奪走了我的獵物，卑鄙無恥！"獅子笑着回答説："難道你是光明正大地從朋友那兒得到這個禮物的嗎？"

這則寓言揭露兇惡、貪婪的強盜，這種人一旦自己遭了殃卻要責罵別人。

149
狗和狼

　　羣狼和一羣狗交戰，狗推選希臘狗為司令，可是它不急着開戰，部下們卻紛紛對它大聲埋怨。狗司令説：“我現在就告訴你們我這麼做的原因。做任何事情都該事先有個計劃。狼的品種和毛色千篇一律，可是我們的狗外貌不同，品種不同，甚至連毛色也不一樣：黑色，褐色，白色，還有灰色。我們之間毫無共同點，意見也都不一致，叫我如何統帥大家去打仗呢？”

團結一致才能戰勝敵人。

小鹿和鹿爸爸

　　一天小鹿對鹿爸爸說："老爸，你天生就比狗個頭兒大，也比狗跑得快，還有兩隻角用以自衛；你為甚麼要怕它呢？"鹿回答說："這些我都知道，不過只要一聽到狗的吠叫聲，我就會頭昏腦漲，只知道逃跑，甚麼也想不到了。"

天生膽小的人，無論看起來多沒高大強壯，即使磨破嘴皮也不能使他英勇頑強。

151
燭台

燭台上的燭心吸足了油，熊熊燃燒起來，於是便開始自吹自擂，說自己的光比太陽還要亮。可是剛颳來一點風，燭火就熄滅了。有個人把蠟燭扶起來說道：“你只管發光，別吭聲，太陽光不會把你遮蓋的。”

不要被榮譽和生命中的輝煌衝昏頭腦；任何財富都不會永遠屬於一個人。

田鼠和家鼠

兩隻老鼠，一隻田鼠，一隻家鼠，互相串門作客。家鼠先到朋友田鼠家去作客，當時田裏的莊稼已經成熟，它一邊啃着田鼠款待自己的麥子和帶土疙瘩的麥茬一邊説：「你的日子過得像螞蟻一樣不幸！我的日子可富裕啦，要甚麼有甚麼，和你相比，我簡直是生活在樂土上！要是你願意的話，就到我那兒去做客吧，我們痛痛快快地美餐一頓！」家鼠説服了田鼠，把它帶到了家裏。家鼠拿出麵包、麵粉、豆子、無花果、蜂蜜、酸棗，一樣樣招待客人，田鼠面對這麼一大堆好吃的東西，欣喜若狂，眼花繚亂。它從籃子裏拿出一塊奶酪，拖到自己跟前。忽然有人開了門；兩隻老鼠立刻逃到一條窄縫裏，吱吱叫着躲藏起來，你擠我，我擠你，好不難受。後來，一隻老鼠探出身子去拿無花果，誰知又有人進了屋，兩隻老鼠只好再次躲藏起來。這時候田鼠雖然肚子很餓，卻對家鼠這麼説：「再見了，雖然你的日子過得看似快活，但這一切卻是靠着日復一日冒險犯難換來的。既然如此，我寧願繼續啃我的麥茬和小草，雖然日子過得簡樸，卻不用擔驚受怕。」

簡樸而安穩的生活勝於提心吊膽地享受奢華。

153
兔子和狐狸

兔子問狐狸：“你真的打獵很精明，被大家稱為狐狸獵手嗎？”狐狸回答說：“要是你不信的話，那就到我這裏來吧，我請你吃一頓大餐。”兔子聽了狐狸的話，可是它一走進狐狸的家，卻讓自己成了狐狸的盤中餐。兔子無可奈何地嘟嚷道：“雖然我沒得到好下場，但是我總算看清楚了你的真面目：你不是狐狸獵手而是狐狸騙子！”

一個人好奇心太重，又不善於掌握分寸，最後往往沒有好下場。

狼和狗

    一羣狼對一羣狗説："我們彼此間甚麼都相像,為甚麼不像親兄弟一樣和睦相處呢?我們之間其實沒有甚麼區別,只不過生活方式不同罷了。我們自由自在地生活,而你們服從人的指揮,給他們當奴隸,為此你們得忍受他們的毆打,脖子上得套上項圈,還要為他們看護羊羣。可是人類給你們吃的東西只不過是幾根骨頭。要是你們聽我們一句,把你們看護的羊羣交出來,那我們就能一起痛痛快快地飽餐一頓了。"狗聽從了狼的勸告,可是狼進了羊欄之後首先撕爛的是狗。

背叛祖國的人都會得到應有的報應。

155
驢子和馬

驢子羨慕馬吃的飼料精美，受的照顧周到，不禁為自己的不幸命運痛哭流涕：自己不得不背負重物，卻總是飢腸轆轆，可是馬頭上戴着韁繩，身上披着馬具，疾馳如飛，好不威風。正當驢子這麼思索的時候，戰爭爆發了。主人全副武裝騎上馬背，朝敵人飛奔而去。馬受到襲擊，遍體鱗傷，倒地而死。這時候驢子改變了原先的想法，並對馬起了惻隱之心。

不要羨慕人家有錢有勢，要看到背後所遭受的蔑視和危險，應該甘於貧窮，因為貧窮是安寧之母。

蛇頭和蛇尾

有一次，蛇尾決定朝前爬，並把身體的其他部分一起帶走。這些部分提出異議：“你怎麼能帶着我們走呢？你既沒有眼睛，也沒有鼻子，跟其他動物不一樣。”可是尾巴不聽話，它覺得自己的想法合情合理。於是，尾巴盲目地向前爬行，把整個身子拖在後面，直到鑽進一個石頭縫裏，弄得遍體鱗傷才罷休。直到這時蛇尾才低聲下氣地請求蛇頭說：“行行好吧，先生，救救我們吧！我現在知道錯了。”

這則寓言揭露那些攻擊主人的陰險狡猾之徒。

157
玫瑰和莧菜

莧菜同玫瑰並排生長，它對玫瑰説："你的花多麼絢麗多姿！上帝也好，人類也好，大家全都喜歡你。啊，我羨慕你的美麗和芬芳！""不，莧菜，"玫瑰回答説，"我的壽命極其短暫，即使大家不採摘，我也會枯萎凋落。而你長生不老，鬱鬱葱葱，彷彿剛剛吐翠的細枝嫩葉。"

一輩子過小康生活勝於短暫的闊綽之後遭受厄運甚至命赴黃泉。

號角手

軍隊裏有個號角手，常常吹着號角召喚大家去和敵人作戰。有一次他被敵人俘虜，他懇求敵人饒他一命，因為他既沒殺過一個人也沒搶過一個人，除了自己負責的那只銅號角，他一無所知。敵人對他説："你召喚其他人去作戰，而不是制止他們出擊，你害死的人更多。"

教唆者比作惡者本人更可惡。

159
受傷的老雕

老雕停在懸崖上窺視着幾隻兔子，打算朝它們撲過去。不料獵人朝它射出一箭，鋒利的箭頭扎進老雕的身子，而帶着羽毛的箭尾則在它的眼前晃來晃去。老雕看了便說：“我感到加倍疼痛是因為我知道將要死於自己的羽毛之下。”

朋友帶來的痛苦令人痛上加痛。

農夫與不結果實的樹

有個農夫家的地裏長着一棵從不結果的大樹,只能給吵吵嚷嚷的麻雀和蟬棲息。農夫覺得這棵不結果實的樹留着沒用,打算砍掉。他掄起斧頭,向樹砍去。蟬和麻雀紛紛向他懇求,讓他別毀了自己的棲身之處,它們願用美妙的歌聲來為他消愁解悶。可是農夫沒有理睬它們,對着大樹砍了第二下、第三下。這時候,樹上出現了一個大窟窿,農夫發現裏邊有一窩蜜蜂和許多蜂蜜。他嚐了嚐蜂蜜的味道,立刻丟下斧頭,從此以後這棵樹就被視為聖樹,得到主人的精心照料。

與其説人類生來就重視、愛好公正,不如説他們天生喜歡追求私利。

161
禿子騎士

有個禿子頭上戴了一個假髮套，耀武揚威地騎在馬上馳騁。忽然，一陣風颳來，吹落了他頭上的假髮，邊上所有看到的人都哈哈大笑。可是這個人卻勒住馬，滿不在乎地說："這有甚麼好大驚小怪的？不屬於我的頭髮飛走了，剩下的正是我出生時的模樣。"

遭到不幸不要傷心，要知道不屬於自己的東西想留都留不住。我們空手而來，空手而歸。

老闆和船員

有個老闆乘船在海上航行，天氣惡劣，他受涼得病。陰雨連綿的日子裏，船員們紛紛前來探視，向老闆伸出援助之手，可他卻對他們説："如果你們不把船開得快一點，我就拿石頭來扔你們！"有一個船員回答："唉，但願我們能到達有石頭的地方！"

我們生活中也是如此：為了免遭大欺凌，不得不忍受一點小委屈。

163
烏鴉和水罐

烏鴉口渴難忍，飛到一個水壺旁邊，試圖將它推倒。可是水壺昂首挺立，一動也不動，烏鴉沒力氣弄倒水壺。不過烏鴉想出了一個妙計，最終達到了目的：它撿起石子往水壺裏扔，當石子積少成多，堆得很高時，裏頭的水就往上湧，往外溢，這樣烏鴉便如願以償地解了渴。

智慧比力量重要。

164
捕鳥人與蟋蟀

這則寓言說的是捕鳥人的故事，告誡我們，面對問題不能只聽其言，也要觀其行。

捕鳥人聽到蟋蟀的叫聲，心想，到手的獵物一定不少，因為他是根據蟋蟀的鳴叫聲來判斷的。可是當他使出所有的本領抓住蟋蟀後，這才發現，除了蟋蟀以外甚麼也沒有，他從此不再相信耳朵聽見的聲音，聲音往往使許多人作出錯誤的結論。

凡事不能只看表面。

165
老馬

有匹馬年老體衰，筋疲力盡，它不得不離開戰場，來到磨坊推磨，不免為自己的不幸痛哭流涕，念念不忘往日的戰鬥生涯。"唉，"馬對磨坊主說，"我曾經馳騁沙場，全身披紅掛綠，好不威風，飲食起居也有專人照料。可現在，我完全不明白自己究竟犯了甚麼錯，非得離開戰場來伺候這些磨盤。"磨坊主答道："別嘮叨過去的事情了，凡夫俗子都是這個命 —— 隨遇而安吧，既要樂於飛黃騰達，也要甘心失意潦倒。"

這則寓言說的是馬的故事，告誡我們要樂天知命。

三頭公牛和一頭獅子

三頭公牛在一起吃草，一頭獅子跟在它們後面，打算向它們進攻。可是三頭公牛彼此和睦相處，形影不離，獅子沒辦法對付它們，於是決定先把它們拆散，然後再各個擊破。獅子挑撥離間，使它們彼此不和，反目成仇。當三頭公牛終於各奔東西，形單影隻時，獅子就輕而易舉地解決了自己原先對付不了的獵物。

這則寓言説的是公牛的故事，告誡我們要齊心協力。

167
獅子和狐狸

狐狸住在獅子那兒,為它東奔西跑,充當助手,專門負責給獅子打探狩獵的地方,然後由獅子親自出馬去襲擊獵物。等到把獵物捕獲回來,它們就論功分贓。結果狐狸當然不滿意,它開始嫉妒起獅子,因為獅子認為狩獵的功勞比狐狸的打探工作更大。因此狐狸試圖自己去襲擊牲口,不料非但沒有捕獲獵物,自己反倒成了獵人的獵物。

這則寓言說的是狐狸的故事,告誡我們做事要量力而為。

橄欖樹和無花果樹

橄欖樹嘲笑無花果樹：“我一年四季開花結果，而你每次季節交替都會花朵凋零。”它剛說完這句話，忽然間大雪從天而降。原本橄欖樹正值花繁葉茂，這下子它的幼枝嫩葉上撒滿了雪花，大雪把橄欖樹的美貌連同自身全都毀了；而無花果樹枝上光禿禿，沒有樹葉，雪花直接降落在地上，絲毫沒有受到傷害。

對於不明智的人來說，美麗會成為恥辱。

169
蜜蜂和牧羊人

蜜蜂在橡樹洞裏釀蜜，正好給一個路過的牧羊人看到。牧羊人起了歹念，打算把蜂蜜佔為己有。不料蜜蜂從四面八方圍上來，拼命往他身上蜇。最後牧羊人無奈地說："我還是走吧，要是為了這點蜂蜜讓我跟蜜蜂較量，那我寧可放棄。"對於利慾熏心的人來說，非分之財是有害之物。

這則寓言說的是蜜蜂和牧羊人的故事，告誡我們不要給壞人可乘之機。

170
老雕、蛇和農夫

蛇和老雕廝殺起來，雙方打得不可開交，蛇盤起身子，眼看就要把老雕一圈圈纏住。一個農夫看到後，用手把蛇掰開，放走了老雕。蛇對此耿耿於懷，在老雕的救命恩人農夫飲的酒中投了毒。農夫絲毫沒有察覺，正打算喝酒，老雕及時趕到，奪去了農夫手中的酒杯。

善有善報。

171
渡鴉和天鵝

這則寓言說的是渡鴉的故事，告誡我們不要違背自然規律。

渡鴉看到天鵝，對天鵝身上的白羽毛感到十分羨慕。它斷定，如果把自己洗乾淨，它也能像天鵝一樣美麗多姿。於是渡鴉離開自己經常覓食的祭壇，開始在水鄉澤國定居下來。可是無論渡鴉怎麼洗也無法改變自己羽毛的顏色，而水邊又沒有自己能吃的食物，最後渡鴉為了追求美麗而送了命。

大自然的規律是不會改變的。

河流與海洋

河流匯聚在一起開始責備海洋："我們把甘甜的淡水送到你那裏去，可是為甚麼我們的水一進入你的懷抱，立刻就變成了苦澀的鹹水，無法飲用？"海洋聽到詆毀它的話，針鋒相對地說："別流到我的水中來，你們就不會變鹹了。"

這則寓言針對那些忘恩負義，對恩人橫加指責的人。

173
公牛、母獅和野豬

公牛看到一頭熟睡的獅子，便伸出牛角去撞它，獅子毫無防備，送了性命。獅子媽媽趕來，為兒子失聲痛哭。野豬看到母獅如此悲痛，便站得遠遠的，說道："唉，不知有多少父母親現在正在為失去孩子而流淚呢，而那些孩子都是被你們獅子給害死的。"

惡有惡報。

174
狗和狐狸

　　羣狗發現了一張獅子皮，你爭我奪，撕扯不休。狐狸看了看它們，說道：“要是這是一隻活獅子的話，恐怕你們很快就不得不承認，它的爪子可比你們的牙齒還要厲害多了！”

這則寓言揭露了社會上總有些喜歡落井下石的人。

175
生病的鹿

有隻鹿重病纏身，躺在草地上起不來。其他動物們紛紛前來探望，每一次探視都要啃掉一些青草，最後把這隻鹿周圍的所有青草都啃得精光。最後鹿雖然身體康復了，卻因為飼料不夠依然丟了性命。

這則寓言說明：結交損友不但得不到好處，甚至會帶來更嚴重的傷害。

野驢和家驢

野驢看到家驢馱着重物，疲憊不堪，便對家驢奴隸般的命運嘮叨起來："瞧，我才是真正的幸運兒，生活無拘無束，不用勞動，也不必為甚麼事操心，整天悠閒自在地在山上吃草。而你，靠主人養活，受盡了奴役，捱夠了沒完沒了的毆打。"這時候，跑來一頭獅子；它沒有走近家驢，因為家驢有人看顧，而是朝着孤零零的野驢張牙舞爪地猛撲過去，把野驢吃下了肚。

這則寓言說明，固執而任性的人希望隨心所欲地生活，然而，沒有別人的幫忙他們很快就會遭到滅頂之災。

177
狗和母狼

狗在追趕一匹母狼，嘴裏自吹自擂，誇自己跑得多麼快，力氣有多大，它以為母狼逃跑是因為沒有它厲害。可是母狼忽然轉過頭來說："我怕的不是你，而是跟在你後面跑的主人。"

這則寓言說明，不要狗仗人勢。

人、母馬和小馬

有個人騎着一匹快要分娩的母馬在路上疾馳，半路上母馬產下一匹小馬。小馬一落地立刻就跟在母親後面跑起來，但很快便累得氣喘吁吁，小馬對騎在馬上的人説："難道你沒看見，我還小，走不了長路？你想想，要是你在這兒把我撇下，我就性命難保；但要是你把我帶走，回到家，然後再好好飼養我，那麼等我長大以後你就能夠騎在我身上到處馳騁了。"

這則寓言説明，應該對那些知恩圖報的人行善。

人和庫克羅普斯

從前有個人，一向為人正直虔誠。長久以來他一直和孩子們一起過着豐衣足食的生活，可是後來他忽然變得非常貧窮。他心裏難過極了，開始詛咒上蒼，並決定了斷此生。他拿了一把寬寬的寶劍，朝一個僻靜的地方走去，覺得一死了之比遭遇不幸、忍受折磨要好。半路上他遇見一個深坑，坑裏有一大堆金子，這是一個名叫庫克羅普斯的巨人藏在那裏的。這個人看到這麼多金子，心裏百感交集，又害怕又驚喜。他立刻扔掉寶劍，從坑裏搬出來許多金子，並帶着金子飛快地回家去見孩子們。後來庫克羅普斯回到自己的坑裏，發現金子不見了，藏金子的地方卻放着一把劍，他二話沒說，拔出寶劍，自刎而死。

這則寓言說明，惡有惡報，善有善報。

獵人和騎士

有個獵人抓到一隻兔子，把它帶在身邊，繼續趕路。半路上他遇到一個騎士，騎士向他要那只兔子，並答應付錢給他。可是騎士一從獵人那兒拿到兔子，立刻策馬疾馳，逃之夭夭。獵人跟在他後面追趕，希望很快就能追上他。當騎上愈跑愈遠時，獵人無可奈何地在他身後呼喊："你走吧！這只兔子算我送給你了。"

這則寓言說明，打腫臉充胖子往往是迫不得已。

181
小偷和旅店老闆

有個小偷住進一家旅店，在那兒一連住了好幾天，指望能偷到一些東西，可是一直找不到機會。有一天正值節日，他發現旅店老闆穿了一件嶄新的紅襯衣坐在旅店門口，附近不見一個人影。小偷走過去，坐在老闆身邊，和他話家常。他們談了整整一小時，隨後，小偷張大嘴巴，像狼一樣嗥叫起來。老闆問他："你這是幹甚麼？"小偷答道："好吧，我告訴你，不過我希望你能答應幫我看好斗篷，我不得不把它留在這兒。善良的先生，我自己也不知道，到底是因為我的罪過呢，還是因為別的原因，我常常會這麼打哈欠。只要我連打三次，就會變成一條狼，向人撲去。"說着，他打了第二次哈欠，並像剛才那樣發出嗥叫聲。老闆聽了他的話之後，以為他說的是實話；他不寒而慄，起身打算逃走。可小偷抓住他的襯衣，開始求他："善良的先生，你可別走，拿着我的斗篷，要不會丟失的！"說着，他張開嘴，開始打第三次哈欠。老闆害怕小偷馬上就要把他吃掉，丟下自己的新襯衣，拔腿就朝旅店裏跑，並且牢牢地鎖上大門。而小偷拿起老闆的新襯衣轉身回家去了。

相信謊言的人常常會自尋煩惱，遭受損失。

愛誇口的甲蟲

一個飽食終日的甲蟲從糞堆裏爬出來，突然看到一隻雕在高空飛翔，而且飛得很快，竟在短短時間內就飛遍了遼闊的天空。甲蟲感到氣惱，對自己的同伴說："你們瞧，這就是雕！它的喙和爪很尖利，身子很強壯，雙翅很快捷，只要它願意，它既能飛上雲霄，也能沖向地面。我和你們卻失寵於大自然，人家既不把我們當作飛禽，也不把我們當作走獸，然而雕的嗓子並不比我的嗓子甜美，羽毛也不比我的鮮豔。不行！我還是想加入鳥類，和鳥一起到處飛翔和生活。"説完，它就飛上了天空，開始發出非常難聽的嗡嗡聲。但是，當它在高空想要跟隨着雕飛翔時，卻擋不住大風的襲擊，它疲憊不堪，驚恐萬分，撲通一聲掉在一個陌生的地方。那裏沒有食物，甲蟲垂頭喪氣地説："飛禽還是走獸都無所謂了，我只求能回到我的糞堆裏。"

目空一切的人們在誇海口時常會遭到懲罰；他們既得不到想追求的那種幸福，還會失去原先擁有的一切。

183
農夫和老黃牛

有個農夫讓老黃牛從牲口棚往外駄牛糞。老黃牛罵他："我
們用自己的勞動為你提供小麥和大麥,讓你和家人們過上
好多年的小康生活,而你的回報卻是要我們幹這種髒活。"農夫
回答:"請問,你們運送的不正是你們自己造出來的東西嗎?""我
們不爭了,"老黃牛們說。"既然這樣,"農夫說,"只有這樣做
才是公正的,休閒時你們弄髒我的房子,上班時就打掃乾淨。"

這則寓言是針對那些傲慢又愛抱怨的僕人。他們只要做了一點
事,就會埋怨,卻忘記了人家為自己做了多少事。然而如果自己
做了蠢事,則絕口不談。

狐狸和月亮的倒影

夜裏，一隻狐狸在河邊遊蕩，看見水中的月亮倒影，便斷定這是乾酪。於是它開始喝水：它認為只要把河水喝光，讓河乾涸就會得到乾酪。因此它不停地喝水，直到被水嗆死。

貪婪的人就是這樣拼命地想要發財，結果卻提前把自己送進墳墓。

185
山羊和狼

狼在追一隻山羊，想要逮住它；但是山羊爬上了河邊一個高高的懸崖，在那裏它是很安全的。狼在下面坐下來候着它。過了一天、兩天、三天，狼終於感到餓了，而山羊則感到渴了，於是，它們朝不同的方向走開了：先是狼去找吃的，後來是山羊去找水喝。山羊喝足了水，看了看自己在水中的倒影，說道："啊，我的腿多麼美，鬍子多麼漂亮，角多麼大呀！狼也敢追逐我嗎？我這就親自走出去見它，不讓它殘害我！"狼從它背後悄悄地偷聽到了這些話，然後猛地用牙齒咬住羊的大腿，並說道："山羊兄弟，你在這裏發表甚麼議論？"山羊看到自己被抓住了，便說道："哎呀，狼先生，請原諒和饒恕我的過錯吧，我們山羊就是這樣，喝足水後，就會開始說些不該說的話。"可是狼並沒有可憐它，而是把它吃掉了。

這則寓言教導無能為力而又一貧如洗的人們不要輕易反抗有權有勢的人。